The Four Horsemen

DEATH

T.A. CHASE

Pride Publishing books by T.A. Chase:

Out of Light into Darkness
From Slavery to Freedom
The Vanguard
Two for One
Where the Devil Dances
Stealing Life

The Four Horsemen
Pestilence
War
Famine
Death

The Beasor Chronicles
Gypsies
Tramps

Home
No Going Home
Home of His Own
Wishing for a Home
Leaving Home
Home Sweet Home

Every Shattered Dream
Part One
Part Two
Part Three
Part Four
Part Five

Rags to Riches Volume One
Remove the Empty Spaces
Close the Distance

Rags to Riches Volume Two
Following His Footsteps
Anywhere Tequila Flows

Rags to Riches Volume Three
Walking in the Rain
Barefoot Dancing

Delarosa Secrets
Borderline
Snap Decision
Cold Truth

The Blood and Thorn Ranch
Bulls and Blood

What's his Passion?
Mountains to Climb
Climbing the Savage Mountain

Anthologies:
Unconventional at Best: Ninja Cupcakes
Unconventional in Atlanta: His Last Client
An Unconventional Chicago: No Bravery
Semper Fidelis: Always Ready
Aim High: Possibilities
Unconventional in San Diego: The Unicorn Said Yes

DEATH

Dedication

Thank you to all the readers who took this journey with The Four Horsemen and me. I appreciate the wonderful words of encouragement, and hope I do Death's story justice. Thanks to my marvelous editor and everyone who had something to do with this story.

Prologue

The crack of gunfire ripped through the lingering fog of the park. It was early enough in the morning no one noticed the noise, except for the four men standing in a clearing. A fifth man lay on the ground, blood staining the white shirt he wore. Two of the four crouched next to the injured man. The other two glanced at each other before the shorter blond man moved toward the threesome. Gatian Almasia turned his back on the others and strolled to where a street urchin held two horses.

"Here."

He flipped the urchin a coin and took taking the reins of the chestnut stallion. After mounting, he settled into the saddle and stared out over the emerging city streets. The fog covering them was burning off, revealing early morning travelers, mostly heading to their jobs in Paris' shops. The man waited for the blond to join him.

"St. Lucian will be dead before the day is over," Du Lauc said softly as he swung astride his own horse.

"Good."

Gatian sounded neither pleased nor saddened by the news. He studied the people moving past him dispassionately. None of them mattered, and they wouldn't, even if he had known their stories.

"Do you think what you did will help your sister? Is anything going to make her forget what happened to her?" Du Lauc asked.

"This is not for her." Gatian waved his hand behind him at the tableau of the two men carrying the other to a waiting carriage.

"Then why do it?"

"Because, Du Lauc, it makes me feel better. That slime will never do to another girl what he did to my sister."

Du Lauc looked at his friend. "Gatian, you could be arrested or exiled for shooting the son of a marquis."

Gatian shrugged, showing no emotion. "It does not matter what they choose to do with me. I have avenged the wrong caused to my sister. Let us go back to my house. I ordered the cook to have a breakfast laid out for us when we arrive."

"Breakfast? How can you think about eating at a time like this? You shot a man." Du Lauc looked horrified at Gatian's calm reaction to the duel.

Gatian twisted in his saddle and grabbed hold of Du Lauc's jacket, yanking the man forward. Gatian curled his upper lip in disgust.

"Do you think I give a whit about St. Lucian? He raped my sister, and that is one thing I will not overlook."

Du Lauc froze under Gatian's cold gaze, yet he couldn't seem to help himself from speaking further.

"You know your sister was not a maiden when St. Lucian had her," he pointed out, taking his life in his hands by suggesting it.

Gatian shoved him away so hard, Du Lauc almost fell off his horse. After facing forward, Gatian tossed another coin to the urchin.

"Run ahead to Almasia House. Tell the butler his master will be following behind you, and he expects hot food and warm drink to be waiting."

"Aye, milord." The boy tucked the coin somewhere safe before sprinting away.

Monsieur Gatian Almasia had no title, and no noble blood running through his veins. Yet he had the one thing people responded to, and that was money. No one knew how Gatian had made his fortune, and he never said a word about how it happened.

To others it may have seemed he had no interest in currying favors from the nobles or other rich members of society. As far as he was aware, no one knew anything about the Almasia family. They had simply appeared one day on the second best street in Paris. He'd heard tell none of the gossips could find out when they'd arrived or where they'd come from, but once the money had started flashing about, the rich people had possibly decided he must be from some obscure noble family. It had quickly became known if someone hurt one of the Almasia family, they hurt them both, and the vengeance was swift and vicious.

Gatian's half-sister, Emilia Almasia, was a beautiful young woman and quite popular with the men. Where her brother struck people as cold and distant, Emilia treated everyone well. The girls who were less popular or less beautiful spread rumors about Emilia, though the ones about her being rather free with her favors seemed to be true.

"I have never held Emilia to the unrealistic standards of society. She may give her favors to whomever she chooses." Gatian shot Du Lauc a piercing glare. "*Give* is the important word. No man may force her and expect to live."

"If she were to say anything to anyone, no one would believe her," Du Lauc commented when they started down the street.

Gatian grunted but said nothing while they rode along. He was not interested in what anyone else would believe. Emilia had told him St. Lucian had raped her, and she'd never lied to him. Why would she, when he allowed her far more freedom than most older brothers or fathers?

St. Lucian's death meant nothing to Gatian. It wasn't like he knew the man, or even cared to know him. Other than Emilia, there was no one Gatian cared about anymore, not since that night three years ago when his entire world had died.

Shaking his head, Gatian refused to think about that night. Guilt ate at him like a sore on his soul. So many things he'd done wrong, and only one person had paid the price for Gatian's arrogance. It wasn't the time to think about it. Gatian managed to blank his mind most of the day. Only during the darkest part of night did the memories and sorrow cut through him.

"Are you joining me for breakfast, Du Lauc?"

His closest associate hemmed and hawed for a minute or two. Gatian didn't care one way or the other whether Du Lauc joined him. He was asking merely to be polite, or to seem polite. Honestly, he would rather spend the morning alone or with Emilia, not listening to the mindless chatter of the man next to him.

"I will have to say no, Gatian. My father has demanded my presence at the family house today. Rich cousins or something coming into the city for the season." Du Lauc snorted in unhappiness.

"Sorry to hear that. I suspect I will see you tonight at Count Ramassium's ball?" Again, Gatian didn't care, but he understood he had to ask.

"Yes, I think we will be arriving later in the evening," Du Lauc informed him.

"I am escorting Emilia tonight, so I am sure we will be arriving early. If we do not meet up there, I will see you at the club later on."

Gatian didn't wait for Du Lauc to answer him. He lifted a hand and steered his horse down the street toward his house. When he stopped in front of the large, rather obnoxiously built building, a groom rushed from around the side of the house to take a hold of the reins. Gatian dismounted and nodded at the groom before walking up the front steps. The door opened, and his butler stood there, head bowed, while Gatian walked past.

"Breakfast has been laid out in the back dining room, sir. Lady Emilia has not rung for a tray yet."

"Leave her be until she does. Have the footmen take some hot water up to my room while I am eating. I would like to bathe before I go out again."

"Yes, sir."

Gatian tugged off his gloves and stuffed them in the hat before handing it to one of the servants. He ran a hand through his hair while he strolled down the hallway to the back dining room. After sitting down, he leaned back slightly, giving the footman to place the plate of food in front of him. A pot of tea was set to one side by his plate, and he nodded when another manservant poured a cup out for him.

He didn't move until after they left the room. Once the door had shut behind them, he picked up the cup and sipped at it. Drinking tea was an odd habit for a Frenchman, but Gatian had learned many strange routines since leaving home at the age of fourteen. The tea he ordered to be brewed for him every morning was a special blend he imported from India, brought to him on one of his many ships.

After the tea, he began eating, ignoring the pile of envelopes and newspapers to his left. Gatian had no interest in invitations and announcements of weddings that seemed to abound during the season of meat markets. Most of the ladies wanted him as their next conquest or as a husband. Little did any of them know he wasn't interested in women, and the only one he liked was Emilia.

"Did you do it, Gatian?"

Gatian looked up to see his sister standing just inside the room, her dressing gown thrown carelessly over her shoulders. Her blonde hair, so unlike his own black, cascaded in curls down her back. Emilia's blue eyes glistened with tears, yet he could see the bruising on her cheek from St. Lucian's fist.

"Yes. You knew I would when I made you tell me what had happened to you." He took a bite of eggs. After chewing, he gestured to the table. "Please, sit and eat something. I know you have not eaten in a day or two. It's over and done with, Emilia. We must look forward."

"It was not you he hit and hurt, Gatian. You were not the one helpless against his superior strength."

Gatian heaved a mental sigh. As much as he loved Emilia, she tended toward the dramatic, and he found it annoying at times. He stood and moved over to where his sister was. After putting his arm gently around her shoulders, he motioned to the table.

"You are right, Emilia dear. I'm an arse. I do not know what it is like to be helpless. Please eat. Remember, though, I did tell you we would practice some things you can do to keep yourself safe. Things men would not think a lady would know."

He pulled out a chair and had her sit. Gatian filled a plate with all her favorites, poured her a cup of tea, and placed it all in front of her. He returned to his place and lifted his fork. His hand shook, and because he didn't want her to notice, he set his fork back down.

Emilia had no idea Gatian had lied to her. He did know what it was like to be helpless. To see something done and know there was nothing he could do to stop it. Yet that wasn't true—if he had been there, he could have prevented the death of the only person he'd truly loved. He'd stood there, knowing he was too late, the guilt rising in him until he'd wanted to crouch and scream.

He clenched his hands into fists, tamping down on the rage and sorrow. Gatian had spent many years fighting the depression swallowing him whole. Winning the battle ensured he had no feeling for anything else. He'd lost interest in other people and how they were getting on in the world.

Only Emilia still held a place in his heart, and he wished she would find a man to marry so he could dower her with most of his wealth. Gatian wanted to disappear and spend the rest of his life wandering the world without having to worry about his sister.

"Du Lauc told me St. Lucian would be dead by the end of the day," he informed Emilia.

She nodded, giving no sign of distress or disgust. Emilia never questioned him as to how he would handle the problem, because she knew what he would do.

"Are you not afraid his family will retaliate against you?"

Gatian snorted. "What can they do to me? Shun me? Make me *persona non-gratis* amongst society? I am not afraid of them."

"What if I am? Do you know how hard it is going to be to find a husband if we are shunned by the important people in Paris?" Emilia pushed some of her food around her plate.

"I do not care. They are only people. None of them are important." Gatian took another sip, secretly wishing he could add spirits to his tea.

Emilia threw her silverware onto the table and stood up with a scream. "I know you do not care about them, or apparently about me. You have no idea how I try to ingratiate myself with those awful harridans."

He shoved his chair back and stood as it hit the floor. Gatian braced his hands on the table and leaned toward his sister. He spoke to her with ice freezing his words.

"Do not ever tell me I do not care for you. I injured a man for you this morning. I shot a bullet into his chest and stood there, watching him bleed because he raped you. I did not do it to save your reputation. I did not do it because I hated the man. I did it for you, Emilia, and you never get to question my love for you again."

Emilia took a step back, her hand pressed to her chest and fear in her eyes. Gatian would never hurt her, but he had never shown her anything about his true nature. What she saw at that moment wasn't the usual façade he showed the rest of the world.

"You care for me like you cared for Oliver?"

Gatian pulled himself up straight, and Emilia must have sensed she'd asked the wrong question. She whirled and raced from the room, scampering away like the hounds of hell followed her. He didn't leave his spot in the room. Gatian was frozen while his heart beat so fast it could possibly explode.

No one had spoken Oliver's name to him since he'd died three years ago. Gatian growled low in his throat and swiped his arm over the table, shoving everything to the floor.

He stalked from the room, ignoring the concerned questions from his butler. He would go and wash up before leaving for the day. He didn't want to lay eyes on anyone, especially his sister.

* * * *

Gatian strolled down the sidewalk, weaving slightly as he walked. He twirled his cane and ignored the startled exclamations of the people he bumped into. What did he care if they didn't like him taking up the sidewalk? It wasn't like he knew them or even would see them in his normal day-to-day life.

He took another swig from his flask before tucking it back into his coat pocket. Gatian paused for a second to lean against a streetlamp and stare at the sky. He couldn't see any stars, not like when he'd lived in India several years ago. He found himself missing the openness of the country, though he had been a city boy most of his life.

"Want to have some fun, mister?"

Turning, Gatian spied a skinny girl with lanky, greasy hair standing just outside the light from the lamp. Her clothes were ripped, and he wouldn't doubt they were dirty. He shuddered. Even if he'd been inclined to sleep with women, she wouldn't have been his first choice.

"No thank you, miss. I'm on my way home tonight." He bowed and moved off.

Gatian continued on but slowly became aware of footsteps following him. He didn't change his stance or in any way act like he knew someone was there. Was it the whore who had propositioned him? Had she decided to rob him instead?

Gripping the head of his cane, he twisted it slightly, getting the blade inside ready to be pulled out. If someone was going to try to attack him, he would make him or her rue the day they'd ever thought he'd be an easy mark.

Gatian glanced ahead and spied a back alley opening approaching on his left. They would rush him as he came abreast of it. Gatian understood that, because he would have done the same thing to a man he intended to attack. He tensed as he came upon the alley, and the flurry of footsteps came up behind him like he thought they would.

He whirled, swinging his cane sword as he went. The shock of the blade slicing through fabric and flesh raced up his arm. Gatian didn't let it stop him as he whipped around, trying to keep his balance while pushing the ruffians away.

"I am not giving you anything of mine," he shouted.

The men kept quiet, and their very silence alerted him this might not be a simple robbery. Gatian fought savagely, pulling every trick from his bag, yet there were too many of them. He found himself herded into the alley and surrounded. Gatian gritted his teeth, wishing he hadn't drunk so much at the club. The liquor slowed his reflexes, and the men got in several hits before they simply overwhelmed him.

Gatian slipped on something wet and went to the ground. There was no way he could protect himself from their boots and the pieces of wood they used like extensions of their arms. Even wrapping his arms around his head didn't help. His ribs cracked and caved under the fierce blows. His bones broke, and something tore inside him.

He bit his lip to keep from crying out. They might kill him, but he wasn't going to give them any satisfaction by yelling or begging. Gatian might die, yet he would do it on his own terms. Rolling onto his back, he grasped his sword and thrust with all his strength, driving the blade deep into the gut of one of the men standing over him. Blood gushed over his arm. He closed his eyes while the warm liquid cascaded down.

Finally, he couldn't fight anymore. Gatian accepted his death when he could feel his strength draining from him. He would die in the dirty alley at the hands of ruffians. He looked up to meet the gaze of the head attacker.

"Why?"

The gap-toothed grin the bastard flashed him chilled Gatian's already cold soul. "Did you really think you'd get away with killing some nob? His family don't like the idea of his being dead."

Ah. St. Lucian's family had found a way to exact revenge. Gatian laughed wetly. He should have anticipated this, since St. Lucian didn't have any problem raping a weaker woman, even though she was placed high in society. The man's family wouldn't wince at the idea of killing another man.

Well, at least Emilia wouldn't have to worry about being shunned anymore, Gatian thought as blackness slowly overcame his vision. She would be a sympathetic figure to society for the most part, and her wealth would help smooth any bumps in the road.

His last thought was of Oliver, and he wished he would be seeing his dead lover soon, but Gatian knew he would be heading to Hell, not Heaven. Oliver had been innocent, and his only sin had been caring for Gatian, not knowing what an utter bastard Gatian was.

* * * *

"Get up. We don't have time for you to lay about."

The voice tore through Gatian's mind, and he jerked straight up, looking around for his opponents. Frowning, he realized he wasn't in the alleyway anymore. The landscape surrounding him was barren like nothing Gatian had seen. He pushed to his feet and turned slowly in a circle.

"Are you done?"

Finishing his circle, he glared at the slender, silver-haired man standing there, his arms folded as he impatiently waited for Gatian to complete his circuit. Staring into the man's blue eyes, Gatian barely swallowed his gasp as he noticed the color filled the entire eye, with no pupil or iris.

"Who are you?" He often found attacking a person got him answers when they were more likely not to reply.

The man snorted. "You may call me Lam. You have been chosen, and I have to show you what your new job is."

"Chosen? Where am I? I have never seen a place like this." He motioned in a vague circle. "How did I get here?"

"You died in a back alley in Paris. Instead of being sent to wherever your judgment called for you to go, you were sent to me. I'm pretty sure you won't like what you're about to do, but it's none of my business. I'm only here to teach you before you are sent out on your own."

Lam whistled, and Gatian jumped when a pale gray stallion appeared out of thin air. The stallion snorted at him like it was saying hello. Gatian reached out to touch the horse's nose. Jerking away from him, the horse shook its head. Obviously it wasn't interested in him petting it.

"This is your horse." Lam nodded in the gray's direction. "Now that you're Death, the Pale Rider, you need a mount."

"Death? Pale Rider?" Gatian repeated, confusion pounding in his head.

Gatian remembered something else that had happened before he'd woken up in this strange place. He stretched, searching for pain or broken bones. Yet nothing had hurt, and there were no wounds or blood anywhere.

"Is there a reason why I have no wounds or torn clothes?" Gatian grasped Lam's arms and shook the man. "Who are you, and why am I not dead?"

Lam didn't respond, and didn't try to break Gatian's hold. He simply studied Gatian with a sardonic twist to his lips. Gatian found he hated Lam, if only for his calm reaction to Gatian's yelling.

When his anger settled back into coldness, he let Lam go and stepped back. He'd never got anything by losing his temper. He tampered all his questions and doubts down deep and rested his hands on his hips.

"Where are we going? And tell me again what a Pale Rider is?"

"Nice try, my friend. I never told you once what a Pale Rider is, except that you're the new one. You are dead, in the most fundamental way possible. You can never go back to your old life, and while all those you know will die, you will continue to live forever." Lam paused and tilted his head. "Or until you forgive yourself of all that guilt you've been carrying around."

"Guilt? What guilt?"

Lam grinned and slapped Gatian on the shoulder. "You can deny it all you want, but I can see it in the set of your shoulders and the chill in your eyes. You did something you regret, and it's been eating at you since it happened. Well, whatever it was, it's brought you to this. As the leader of the Four Horsemen, you will be in charge of keeping the world in balance."

Gatian shrugged. "I have no idea what you are talking about. Who are the Four Horsemen?"

"Climb on your horse and come with me. I have a lot to teach you and a short window of time to do it in." Lam motioned to the gray stallion.

Should he go? Was this some sort of trick Gatian's brain was playing on him? Could he be alive but caught in his head somehow? Gatian swung astride the stallion and smiled at Lam.

"Lead the way, Lam. I am sure you will answer all my questions in due time."

Lam narrowed his eyes at Gatian like he understood Gatian wasn't satisfied. Gatian kept his expression bland, not willing to give anything away. With a nod of Lam's head, they disappeared.

Chapter One

The room swirled with colors, bright and dark. Reds and blacks mingled with purples and greens. Pierre giggled as he lay on the floor of the hotel room, his eyes barely focusing on the actual furniture or the ceiling. The heroin raged through his veins, dragging his brain down into a drugged fog. He couldn't remember how long he'd been in the room.

Had it been an hour, a day, or several days? Time rushed by at the speed of light, and yet the seconds crawled. He'd injected the drug into his arms and legs every time the thrill began to wear off. Pierre didn't want to think about what had brought him to Paris and why he was alone in the hotel instead of wandering the streets. Being who he was made it easy to have the drugs delivered, and the people who brought it to him didn't care how much he had as long as he paid them.

"I do believe I might be hungry," Pierre shouted to the empty room.

Was he hungry or had some random thought skated across his mind that he should be hungry? How long had it been since he'd eaten anything? He guessed it depended on how long it had been since he'd arrived at the hotel. Pierre had eaten in the hotel restaurant before returning to the room and discovering his wonderful dream come true had disappeared into reality.

It was the moment he'd dropped the note when he'd called for the drugs to be delivered. No one had questioned him, and certainly no one had stopped him. Not when there was a cash cow living in the penthouse suite, spending thousands of dollars a day and asking nothing but for them to allow the dirty, lank-haired man to go up there once in a while.

A noise caught Pierre's attention and he rolled his head over to one side. He found himself staring at a pair of shoes. *Italian leather,* he thought. They were beautifully made, and Pierre bit back the envy swelling inside him. Silly really, when he could have bought a hundred pairs just like them.

"Are we sure this is the right one?"

He trailed his gaze up from the shoes over the tailored black slacks and black linen shirt. His mouth fell open when he looked into the eternally black eyes of the most handsome man he'd ever seen. Everything about the man spoke of darkness, and falling into a pit without hope of climbing back out.

"As sure as I can be. The orders have never been wrong before."

Turning his head again, Pierre blinked at the sight of the two strangers embracing. Where the first man was darkness and sadness, the second man was lightness and happiness. His silver hair gleamed in whatever light shone through the windows. The blond's eyes were as blue as the daytime sky.

"He doesn't look like someone Gatian would go for," the dark one commented, nudging Pierre with the toe of his expensive shoe.

The light one snorted. "I'm not sure what type Gatian would have gone for, but over the centuries, he hasn't shown any interest in any of the men he came across. There must be something about this particular one that makes him special."

"I guess. Well, what do we need to do to ensure he comes to find this creature?"

Pierre would have blushed if he had the energy, and the drugs didn't cloud his thought process. As it was, he could make out the disgust in the dark one's voice, but he had no shame left. He reached out toward the blond.

"Who are you?" He barely managed to ask the question.

"Don't touch him. I bet he hasn't bathed in a week." Italian Loafer Dude curled his upper lip in disdain.

"Silence, Day. We aren't here to judge him. That will come when his life is over." The other one crouched down. "You may call me Lam."

Day grunted. "Looks like his death will be sooner than anyone anticipated."

"Hush, Day. Keep your opinions to yourself. It's none of our business why this one was chosen for him. We have to make sure he'll stay alive long enough for Gatian to come and get him."

Lam brushed his hand over Pierre's forehead. Pierre whimpered as he started to shake. He didn't know how long it'd been since his last hit, but it felt like the high was wearing off. His eyes rolled in their sockets, and he wanted to plead with Lam to get him some more.

"What do we do with him now? He's going to go into withdrawals, and once that happens, it won't be pretty." Day tapped his foot on the floor next to Pierre's head.

"My orders are to make sure Gatian gets here in the next day or two. So Pierre needs to stay alive until then, at least, but he can't do that if he's not high." Lam shook his head. "You'll have to call his dealer and get more heroin delivered."

"You're an angel," Pierre murmured before he began coughing. His insides twisted, and his stomach tried to crawl out of his throat. He curled into a fetal position, wrapping his arms around his legs and crying out as pain ripped through every inch of his body.

"How did you know?" Lam joked with a smile.

"I'm not the boy's dealer, Lam. I refuse to buy drugs for him, or call someone to come and bring it to him." Day sounded angry.

Pierre didn't care who brought what. He simply needed heroin, or something to dull the pain.

"He needs to have the heroin, and you need to make sure he gets it," Lam ordered. "You know this, Day. If you weren't going to help me, why did you agree to come with me?"

"Because I rarely get time with you. To have more time, I would agree to visit the Master himself."

Pierre rolled over onto his back when his entire body seized. His legs and arms drummed the floor while his head banged against the carpet as well. Foam formed around his lips, and he couldn't breathe anymore. He was dying and it hurt far worse than he'd ever imagined.

"Day, just get the stupid stuff. He can't die right now."

Lam didn't touch Pierre, but for some reason just Lam's presence seemed to ease some part of Pierre's soul. Pierre lost track of time while his fit continued. All his brain could focus on was the pain and the need clawing at his veins. God, he wanted to slice open his skin and let the fire burning in his flesh out. He hated withdrawal symptoms, having discovered how bad they were the year before when he'd gone through rehab the first time.

"Fine."

Pierre smelled sulfur for a faint second, and Lam sighed.

"I do wonder why I stay with him at times. He's very stubborn."

"Because you love him," Pierre managed to say through chattering teeth. He'd reacted to the emotion in Lam's voice.

"True, but that leaves us both in a very precarious situation." Lam sounded unhappy.

"Sorry," Pierre whispered.

He moaned when Lam's cool hand landed on his cheek. Pierre forced his eyes open and stared up into Lam's blue eyes. While there was sadness in the bright fields of color, Pierre saw peace in them as well. He wanted to reach up to touch Lam's pale skin. Unfortunately, he had no strength to lift his arms.

Pierre lay on his back, panting while the pain eased for a moment. A sudden thought hit him, and he frowned.

"How did you get in here? Did I somehow leave the door open? But I don't remember leaving the room."

"Don't worry about how we got here. Just concentrate on living." Lam brushed aside his questions.

"But I would rather die than live," Pierre admitted to the silver-haired man kneeling next to him. He'd never spoken those words aloud before.

Lam cupped his face and smiled gently at him. "Hang on, Pierre. I promise help is coming, and in a day or two, someone will arrive to take you away. You have to be strong even after he retrieves you. Gatian isn't a bad man."

A snort came from the balcony, and they both looked over to see Day standing there. The dark man tossed some things down next to Lam's knee.

"Here you go. I never thought I'd become some human's dealer. There's enough in there to get him through a day or two, and a bag of tainted stuff. He'll need to take that to bring Gatian here, per your orders."

Pierre wrinkled his nose at the stronger scent of sulfur. "What smells like rotten eggs?"

Day heaved an annoyed sigh. "I'm getting very tired of that. Are you ready to go, Lam? I'm sure he can figure out how to shoot up. Hell, he's probably been shooting up for years."

"Did you make sure to get clean needles at least?" Lam shoved to his feet and nudged the heroin closer to Pierre.

"Seriously? You're worried about him catching something from dirty needles?" Day shook his head. "Don't worry, Mom. I got him clean needles as well."

Pierre blinked as Lam kissed Day, and if he wasn't trying to figure out how to stay alive long enough to prepare the heroin before plunging the needle into his arm, he'd get hard at the sight. *So pretty*, he thought.

"Let's go. We'll make sure Gatian gets here in a day or two. The timing has to be just right. Pierre must be on the edge of death, but shouldn't have died yet." Lam wrinkled his nose.

"He'll take care of it, I'm sure." Day stared at Pierre, his dark eyes burning with intense fire. "You never saw the two of us. Trust me, it would be a painful punishment if you talk about this."

Pierre nodded, not really understanding what Day talked about. The warning wasn't necessary, considering Pierre was pretty sure the whole incident was his imagination. Within a blink, Day and Lam were gone, and Pierre didn't worry about the two men.

He scrabbled with the needles and bags, cooking up the heroin and filling the syringe with his drug of choice. Then the tiny burn of pain when the needle went into the vein on his left arm. The strangest sensation of the heroin slipping into his blood caught his attention. This was what he lived for now, and God, how much did he love this.

When the needle was empty, Pierre slumped on the floor and sighed. A wave of well-being swelled over him, and euphoria crashed down into his body. Every atom in Pierre's body relaxed, and he smiled. *Perfect* rippled through his mind. It didn't matter if the man he thought loved him had abandoned him.

Nothing mattered anymore while he surfed the tide of the dragon's fire burning through his veins.

* * * *

Pierre peered down at the bag in his hand. It was the last packet of heroin Day had brought him, or whoever had got the drug into his room. Should he call for more to be delivered before he shot up the last bunch?

His hands shook, and he dropped the baggie. It fell to the carpet beside his feet, and he sat there, staring at it. How had it got there? Had he dropped it or had it always been there?

He slid down off the bed onto the floor and scooped up the baggie, clutching it to his chest. Pierre glanced around the room, searching each shadow. Since the night before, he'd been sure someone had been watching him. Of course, his rational mind knew there wasn't anyone in the room with him, but the paranoia demanded he pay attention to it.

No. He'd shoot up the last batch and order more when he started to come down off it. Pierre licked his dried lips, need starting to gnaw into his flesh. Undoing the baggie, he placed the lump into his spoon and put a few drops of water over it. He stirred it a little to make sure it didn't stick to the surface.

Pierre picked up his lighter and began cooking the heroin. He wanted to make sure it was all dissolved into the water. The brownish liquid floated in the spoon, and his hands shook in anticipation.

His little kit held several cotton balls, and he used one to soak up all the liquid. After that was done, he took his syringe to pull up the entire drug. Pierre could have done this in his sleep, and in many ways, he was. The craving and desire built inside him. His heart pounded, speeding up his breathing. God, he wanted the heroin flowing through his blood as quickly as possible.

As soon as the syringe was full and all the air bubbles tapped out, he tied the tourniquet around his arm. He hadn't used his right arm for the last day or two, so the vein should be fine. Everything was done, and he pressed the end of the needle into his flesh. Pierre pushed the plunger, and the heroin entered his bloodstream with a rush.

It was only when fire ripped through his arm that Pierre realized there must be something wrong with the heroin he'd gotten. How could that be? All the other lumps were fine. Actually, it had been some of the best shit he'd ever gotten. Maybe it came from being in Paris. Could be they got the good shit.

Every inch of Pierre's body stiffened, and he thought his heart stopped for a moment. It started beating again, pounding so hard he believed it would rip open his chest and fly out. He slumped against the side of the bed, his hands hitting the floor. He couldn't move as he tried to rip the needle out of his arm. Yet there was nothing left in the syringe. He'd shot it all, and the corrupted drug was eating him alive.

Foam framed his mouth, which seemed so odd, considering how dry his mouth and throat were. He tried to shout or make some noise for people to come find him. Another stupid idea because there was no way anyone would come looking for him. At least not for another day or so, since he'd paid up through the rest of the week for the suite. Pierre had put a Do Not Disturb sign out when he'd first arrived, and there had been no maid service.

Pierre listed to one side, not having any ability to brace himself, and felt his head rebound off the carpet. *Shit!* It was going to leave a bruise. He closed his eyes, and his arms flailed all around him as the seizures started. At some point, he was sure his heart would stop, and he'd die in the penthouse of a Paris hotel. God, he didn't want to prove his father right, or at least, the man he'd always assumed was his father. Yet did it matter in the long run? No one had ever cared about him or what he was doing. They all threw money at him without stopping to ask him if it was what he wanted.

Now wasn't the time to whine about his life. Pierre should be worried about getting someone's attention to save him. While he thought about crying out again, nothing worked on his body. He could feel his life disappearing, and there wasn't anything he could do about it. The drug slashed through him like razor blades, shredding his insides. His throat clenched shut until he could no longer breathe.

Panic gave him strength as he scratched at his throat. Air! He needed air to stay alive. Something told him it wouldn't work out for him. This was going to be the end, and did he have anything to show for his life? Pierre didn't think he even had any friends who truly liked him. The people who hung around him wanted the money he had, or to meet the people he knew. They didn't care about who he really was.

"What is going on here?"

Pierre jerked. Well, maybe he twitched at the sudden sound of the voice. It wasn't like he had the ability to jerk, sit up, or anything else. Everything else involved breathing, and since he was pretty sure he wasn't inhaling or exhaling, Pierre figured he wasn't moving.

"Why did I get sent here to pick up a junkie who overdosed on some bad stuff?"

Forcing his eyes opened, Pierre stared up into the all-black eyes of a stranger. He blinked, trying to focus on the image in front of him. Christ! He swore he'd seen eyes that color before, but when and where? It shouldn't have been something he'd forget.

The gray-haired man grimaced before taking a seat on Pierre's bed. "Since when am I sent to gather one single soul?"

Pierre dragged one of his hands across the floor and touched the man's foot, which was shod in expensive Italian leather. Yet another item Pierre remembered seeing lately, but were those images real or delusions?

"Could you not touch me? I don't think you've showered in days, maybe even a week or so." The man drew his foot away, out of Pierre's reach.

"Who are you?" Pierre forced between clenched teeth and desert-dry lips.

"Does it really matter who I am?" The man's gray hair seemed to shimmer in the sunlight drifting through the gap in the curtains.

Pierre had never seen hair exactly that color. Oh, he'd seen gray hair before, but none of the ones he'd seen gleamed like tarnished silver. "It might. What's your name? Mine is Pierre."

"Really? Are we being polite now?"

Pierre shrugged at the man's sarcastic question. He took a deep breath and shock rippled through him. The dying didn't seem to be happening anymore. Of course, he might be dead already, and all of this could be nothing more than an after-death experience.

"I guess I can tell you. I'm Death, and I've come to escort you to the gates." Death stood and bowed gracefully to Pierre.

"Are you kidding? Death? Seriously?" Pierre coughed as pain began to tear through him again. Whatever peace or euphoria he might have got from the heroin had disappeared, and he was back to dying.

Death sat again and shook his head. "Apparently you are going to die, and for some odd reason, I've been sent here to take you in for judgment. I'm not sure why they would waste me on just one soul, but I don't ask questions anymore. It tends to be frustrating when no one answers them."

Pierre slapped Death's leg, trying to get the man to help him, or at least to call someone to come and save him. Death leaned forward and pressed two fingertips to Pierre's forehead. The pain eased slightly, though Pierre understood it wasn't gone, and he was still going to end up dead.

"Why are you here?" Death waved a hand at the room. "Seems to me a guy like you could find something better to do than to get strung out in a hotel room."

"A guy like me?" Pierre gasped, forcing air into his burning lungs. He didn't want to suffocate, but he knew his heart was going to stop beating soon. Or maybe explode from beating too fast.

Death tilted his head, studying Pierre for a few minutes. "You might be handsome, after you clean up. Wash all the stench of sweat and drugs from you, and I'm sure someone would go for you."

Pierre wrinkled his nose. "Being handsome doesn't mean anything. I've found it simply means they want to be my friend because I'm pretty, not because I'm a good guy or smart or anything like that."

Death laughed, and Pierre shivered. Death's chuckle was cold and impersonal, giving Pierre the impression Death didn't really find anything amusing. So the man wasn't laughing at him in particular.

"Must be difficult to not be taken seriously." Death shook his head.

Choking, Pierre wrapped his hand around his throat as his airway was restricted again. He coughed and fell onto his side on the floor, bringing his legs up to his chest as tightly as he could. The pressure of his thighs against his body seemed to help keep his heart in place, instead of clawing its way out.

When the fit was over, he flopped over onto his back, staring at the ceiling. What Death had done to him must have slowed down the dying process, but it hadn't stopped it. His strength slowly leaked from him, and it would only be a short time before Death took him to wherever the gates were.

"I was supposed to meet someone here. He said he loved me and wanted to spend a romantic week in Paris." Pierre waved a hand in a vague gesture toward the window. "What city is more romantic than Paris? Well, Rome or Florence might be, but I've never been there before."

"So your lover never came?"

Something in Death's voice made Pierre look at him.

"You've probably heard several versions of the story over the years, huh? I shouldn't have trusted him. I might be rich and good-looking, but I don't have a lot of experience with guys who actually want to spend time with me on our own. Anyway, when I got here, he never showed up, and then I got a picture from a so-called friend of the guy with some girl at a party. I guess he either forgot about me or he never really cared about me to start with."

Pierre closed his eyes and inhaled sharply. He didn't want to whine or make Death pity him. He simply wanted to inform the man of what had happened. Something hitting him in the leg got him to open his eyes. He grunted as a bright light filled the room. Pierre couldn't lift his arm to cover his face.

"Look at me."

He forced his watering eyes to meet Death's dark gaze. The gray-haired man studied him closely before scrubbing his hand over his face.

"I can't believe it," Death muttered. "Is this my chance to rectify what I did wrong?"

Pierre frowned. "What are you talking about? What do you have to fix? You weren't the one who left me here by myself, knowing that I was only six weeks out of my second rehab."

"Six weeks out of your second rehab? Guess the first one didn't stick, huh?" Death grimaced before heaving a sigh. "Well, whether it's a chance to redeem myself, or the opportunity to help you, I don't know, but I suspect I'll be taking you with me."

"Wait," Pierre protested. "I'm not ready to die. I'll give up the drugs and turn my life around if you'll just give me a second chance."

"Bargaining with Death never works," Death informed him. "There is nothing you can offer to stop me from taking your soul, if I want to do so."

Pierre laughed weakly. "It was worth a try. It's not like anyone will miss me if I die."

"Were you trying to commit suicide?" Death glared at him. "Killing yourself isn't the way to solve your problem."

"It wasn't like I planned this. I just wanted to ease the heartache, I guess. It's not like I can get a bad batch of heroin on purpose. You have to work really hard to do that, since most dealers won't admit they cut their drugs with shit."

Death rolled his eyes. "I didn't really mean the bad batch you got this last time, but the whole shooting heroin for over a week or so."

Pierre blinked at him. "Has it really been that long?"

Chapter Two

Snorting, Death stood and started to pace along the perimeter of the room. Pierre stayed on the floor, rank and dirty. Death wrinkled his nose at the stench of the room and Pierre each time he went by the man. Christ! Why couldn't Pierre have taken a shower or four during all the time he was getting high?

"Yes, it's been a week or so, I believe, since you went on your binge." Death folded his arms over his chest and glared out the window. "I'm still not entirely sure why I'm here. I don't do single souls. I am usually called to take large amounts of the dead to the gates."

"Excuse me for not being important enough to rate having Death himself take me alone," Pierre groused.

"Stop whining," Death ordered.

He needed to think. When he gazed into Pierre's eyes he saw they were bright green with flecks of gold. They had been filled with so much pain, and it wasn't just from the bad drugs. Had being abandoned by the man destroyed something in Pierre? Was he so broken inside that all he wanted was to end it? Could Pierre have been so upset he thought killing himself was the best policy?

Yet it wasn't really the pain in Pierre's eyes that caught Death's attention. It was the color so familiar to him in his memories. He might have been alive for centuries and had forgotten his sister's image, but there was one person he'd never forgotten. He'd never allowed himself to let those images and memories fade. Eyes like Pierre's, staring up at him in the throes of passion, and those same eyes looking into the sky, blank and empty of any life.

Death scrubbed his hands over his face and heard Pierre coughing as the pain grew too strong. He had to make a decision. Should he take Pierre to the gates like he was supposed to? Or should he move Pierre to his own residence in the Latin Quarter of Paris? Death could take care of him, and maybe atone for what he'd done to Oliver.

He didn't expect to get the same opportunities as the other former Horsemen, and being absolved of guilt wasn't something he figured would ever happen to him. Forgiveness wasn't something he could give himself, though he knew Oliver would never have blamed him for anything that happened to him.

"Are you a whore?"

Pierre gasped, and Death flinched. There was probably a more politically correct way of asking the question, but Death really didn't care about Pierre's feelings. It wasn't like he was Pierre's best friend or anything.

"Why would I sell myself? My family has money, and I don't need to make any."

The faint lie coloring Pierre's words told Death the truth. He turned to lean against the windowsill and looked down at Pierre.

"Lying to me won't change anything," he pointed out. "I don't really care if you did or not. I was simply asking."

Pierre closed his eyes, obviously not proud of himself, but Death wasn't going to judge Pierre for what he'd done.

"Yes, I have accepted money for sex." Pierre exhaled harshly. "I don't understand why it matters, though."

Death breathed deeply through his nose and gritted his teeth. *Christ!* He should just turn his back and let someone else handle this death, yet no one else seemed to be coming for this soul.

"So you're a whore and a drug addict," Death muttered. "It doesn't surprise me you ended up here, though I would have thought a gutter somewhere would be a more fitting end for you than a penthouse at an expensive hotel."

"Fuck you." It appeared Pierre didn't have the strength to make his voice more than a whisper.

"I must say, you're being rather a bastard, Gatian."

Death started when Oliver's voice echoed through his head. It had been centuries since he'd heard or seen the man. He rubbed his hands over his face. Pierre reminded him of his lover, and how Oliver's life ended because of his arrogance.

While Death thought about Oliver, Pierre started to have another seizure. If he did his job, he'd wait until Pierre's heart had stopped before taking his soul to be judged by someone more knowledgeable than he. Yet in Death's mind, an image of Oliver suffering the same fate plagued him, and Death found he wasn't able to let Pierre die just yet. He needed to figure out why the young Frenchman affected him so deeply.

Death crouched and gathered Pierre in his arms. When he straightened, he sniffed. The scent of cinnamon and sulfur drifted on the breeze, and he tensed.

"Where are you going with him?"

He turned to face Lam with a slight sneer on his face. "Do you really think you have any right to question my actions? What will happen when the others find out who you hang out with?"

Lam grimaced. "It's none of your business, and I was simply asking. I don't really care what you do with the man, but shouldn't you think about your actions a little more? You aren't supposed to save them. You're supposed to let them die so you can take their souls to judgment."

Lam was right, but Death didn't care. If his immediate superiors cared, they could do something about it. It wasn't like he loved being Death. Hell, he could do without all the dead people. He lifted his shoulder in a slight shrug and frowned. Maybe being the messenger angel who worked the closest to the Horsemen, Lam would be able to get the Higher Powers to let Death go for the breach of protocol.

"I'm taking him with me. Maybe he doesn't have to die and I can help him."

Shock rippled over Lam's face, and the messenger angel seemed confused. "Are you a doctor? Or were you a doctor in your former life? I guarantee getting this one off the drugs is going to be a miracle. I think he has a death wish."

"Don't we all?" Death raised his eyebrows at Lam.

Pierre shook so hard Death almost lost hold of him. He glared at Lam and hitched the slender man higher up in his arms. Pierre's head rolled on Death's shoulder, his shallow breaths washing over Death's skin. He tightened his grip, trying to ignore his body's reaction to the closeness of the human.

It didn't seem to matter that Pierre reeked of sweat and illness. Death still found the man attractive in a way he hadn't found anyone in centuries. He wanted to drop Pierre into Lam's arms and run the other way.

But I don't run from anyone.

Snarling, Death shook his head and tried to ignore the voice. He straightened his shoulders and met Lam's intrigued gaze. "I'm taking him with me, and if anyone has a problem, they know where to find me."

"True. Good luck. I think this one's going to be very difficult for you." Lam reached out to stroke his fingers over Pierre's cheek. "He is rather pretty."

Pierre shifted slightly, and Death noticed the man's eyes were halfway open.

"Where's the guy who smells bad?" Pierre asked, staring at Lam.

"I don't know what you're talking about." Lam patted Pierre's cheek before stepping away. "You should probably get him out of here. I'm sure the hotel will be around at some point to make sure he's still alive."

"And they'll panic when he's not here." Death curled his lip in disgust. "They don't care what he does as long as he pays his bill. They don't care about the drugs being delivered or shot up. Why doesn't anyone care about him, Lam?"

Lam blinked, probably amazed Death would even ask the question. "Oh, there are people who care about him, Death, but he doesn't know them yet. Maybe, if he were to live, he'd have met them eventually. Of course, if you're taking him, he might have a chance to find someone who loves him."

Death rolled his eyes and walked over to the balcony. He shouldered the doors open, making sure Pierre got through without getting scraped. Whistling loudly, he eased to the corner, knowing there would be enough space for his horse to appear. The pale gray stallion shimmered as he materialized onto the balcony.

"Wow. I don't usually hallucinate horses appearing out of thin air," Pierre murmured.

"Guess the shit you shot up was worse than you thought," Death said as he waited for Lam to join them. "Here. Hold him for me."

Lam took Pierre while Death mounted his stallion. The horse snorted as Death accepted Pierre back into his arms. Lam chuckled.

"Even your horse is amazed you'd do anything like this."

"Shut up, Lam. If you truly have a problem with me taking him, then just say it or do something about it. You *can* stop me." Death drew Pierre close to his chest. "What are you going to do?"

"Nothing. I didn't see anything here, so I have no idea what you're talking about." Lam turned his back and started to walk into the room. He paused at the doorway and said, "Be careful with him, Death. He's far more fragile than you think. His problems stem from more than just the drugs."

"It's always more than just drugs," Death muttered as he took a tighter hold on Pierre before he nudged the stallion's sides with his heels.

The horse tossed his head up and down for a moment, then whirled on its hind legs. It took one giant leap over the railing, but instead of falling, it raced across the sky, flying without wings. Death didn't touch the reins or grab a handful of mane. He was used to the way his mount traveled. He cupped the back of Pierre's head and pressed the man's face into his chest. He didn't want Pierre looking around, which could cause Pierre to freak out, though Pierre might just assume he was still high and tripping with the bad heroin.

"Have I died yet?"

Pierre's question blew by Death's ears on the night breeze. Death shook his head, not bothering to look down at Pierre.

"If I haven't died, then where are you taking me?" Pierre started to move, but Death stopped him.

"You probably shouldn't look down, or move for that matter. I'm taking you someplace where we can wean you off the drugs. Hopefully, you'll stay clean this time."

"Oh, so you're taking me to a rehab center?" Pierre shrugged. "I guess I could give it another try. It obviously didn't take the first two times."

"How are you feeling?"

Why did he ask? Why was he doing any of this? It wasn't like he knew Pierre or even cared what happened to the human. He should have just walked away and let Lam take the man's soul. Yet he couldn't guarantee Lam would do the job, plus Death could get into trouble for not doing what he'd been chosen for.

Death snorted softly. He'd never turned away from anything asked of him. He'd been furious when he'd woken up and realized he wasn't dead, but stuck in some kind of never-ending limbo.

"He reminds you of me, and you want forgiveness for your failures." Oliver's voice skipped through his thoughts.

"No." Death gritted his teeth. "I can't get forgiveness from you because you're dead."

"Who are you talking to?"

As the last word escaped Pierre's mouth, the human stiffened again, and this time the seizure was severe. It took all of Death's considerable strength to keep Pierre in his arms and on the horse. The stallion huffed in annoyance but landed on the roof of the building Death owned. Death dismounted as quickly as he could, unconcerned with grace or appearances.

He laid Pierre on the rooftop, kneeling next to him with a frown on his face. He didn't know how to fix the problem. Well, he did know one way, and he wasn't going to do that. He wasn't going to go and buy drugs for Pierre. Not when the reason he'd taken Pierre in the first place was to help him get off the heroin.

"Why didn't you do this for me? You promised me you would be there, and you weren't. Why weren't you there?"

Death shook his head. Why was Oliver haunting him now? Why hadn't the man come to him right after he'd died? What was causing him to imagine Oliver's voice in his head? It wasn't like he'd taken any of Pierre's drugs. He doubted he could get high, even if he did shoot heroin.

There was no response he could give to the imaginary Oliver. He had no good reason for why he hadn't been there when Oliver had needed him all those centuries ago. Of course, at the time, he hadn't realized what Oliver meant to him, and how much Oliver's death would come to damage an essential part of his soul.

"Here."

A baggie of syringes and what looked like heroin dropped to the roof next to his knee. Death looked up with a snarl to see Day standing beside him. Surging to his feet, Death made sure he put himself between Pierre and Day.

"You don't get him," Death warned.

Day lifted his hands and took a step back. "Trust me, man, I don't want him. I brought you some stuff because, if you're not going to take him to the hospital, he's going to die. You need to give him some more, and then figure out how to wean him off the shit."

"Why do you care?"

"Why do you? I've never seen you go out of your way to help any of the souls you take for judgment." Day shrugged and turned to walk to the edge of the balcony. "I have my reasons for doing this, and none of them are to get this human's soul. I have millions trying to become my best friend. This skinny druggie doesn't even hit the top of my list."

"Get out of here." Death took a threatening step toward Day. "I don't want your tainted ways around here. Isn't it bad enough you've corrupted a messenger angel? Do you wish to stain someone else who might not be destined for your world?"

Day straightened, anger flashing in his dark eyes, and pushed into Death's personal space. He stuck his finger into Death's chest with a vicious growl.

"Don't ever assume you know me and why I do what I do. If I wished, I could wipe you off the face of this earth and not think twice about it. You aren't untouchable or invincible, Pale Rider. Remember that." Day motioned to Pierre with a dismissive wave. "Do with him what you want. I'm done wasting time."

Within in a blink of Death's eyes, Day was gone, and Death had the strangest feeling that he'd hurt the creature. Yet Day was the most reviled being in the entire universe, being the fallen angel who had defied God. How could anything Death said or did hurt Day in any way? It didn't make sense.

A rasping cough and strangled scream brought Death's attention back to Pierre. Dropping back down to the man's side, Death ground his teeth when he realized Day was right. Pierre's body wasn't strong enough for him to go cold turkey and quit the drugs at once. They risked it being too big a shock to his system.

Since his entire goal was to keep Pierre alive, he had to do something quick.

He reached out and shook Pierre's shoulder. The human flopped like a dead fish, and Death wrinkled his nose. *Shit!* Was he going to have to get the heroin ready for him? When Death was human, people smoked opium or snorted tobacco, but they didn't inject anything into their veins. With his inexperience, he could end up killing Pierre purely by accident.

"Come on, Pierre. You need to wake up a little. Do you want more heroin?"

At the mention of heroin, Pierre's eyelids fluttered. *Should have known the prospect of more drugs would get Pierre moving.* Death inhaled sharply. He couldn't do anything if he continued to complain about it.

He slapped Pierre hard, rocking the man's head back. Death grimaced as a red handprint appeared on Pierre's face, but it must have worked because Pierre opened his eyes and stared up at Death.

"What?"

The word sounded like it had crawled out of Pierre's throat, tearing flesh as it went. Death picked up the bag and tossed it on Pierre's chest.

"Here. If you want the pain to stop, you're going to have to cook the shit up for yourself. I don't ever want to know how to get the heroin ready for you." Death scooped Pierre up in his arms. "Let's get you inside before you do this. I would prefer you not trip out on the roof, in case one of my fellow apartment dwellers chooses to come up here for some night air."

Pierre blinked so fast, Death thought his eyelids might fall off. Obviously Pierre wasn't processing Death's words quickly enough. Death wanted to slap himself upside the head. Did he really think a strung-out junkie would be able to put words together enough to understand anyone?

He shut up and carried Pierre into the living room, where he set him on the couch. Pierre slowly slumped to his side, not having the strength to keep himself upright. Death helped him slide off the couch, onto the floor where he sat, propped up against the furniture. He handed Pierre the bag and started to walk off.

"What? Where are you going?" Pierre tried to lift his arm, but it dropped like it was made of lead.

"I'm not going to sit here and watch you shoot up. Also, I'm not going to cook your drug of choice for you. I have been many things during my long life, but a drug dealer isn't one of them." Death nodded toward the stuff in Pierre's lap. "I'm sure everything you need is there."

"But wait. I can't get the bag open." Pierre did look like he was struggling.

Death stomped back and snatched up the baggie. There was a spoon, lighter, syringes and smaller baggies of brown heroin. There was a white piece of paper in with all the things. Death pulled it out and unfolded it.

"Make sure to give him the heroin marked 'A' first. All the drugs are labeled, and the amounts decrease as you go along. He'll still have withdrawals, but don't let him do more than one hit a day," he read aloud. Death imagined Day snickering as he'd written the note.

"This still doesn't seem like a good idea, but we'll give it a try." He gathered up the heroin, except for the one marked 'A'. That one he tossed at Pierre. "I guess you use this one first. I'll hide the rest of them so you're not tempted to use them all at once."

"But shouldn't you take me to the hospital or something?" Pierre asked.

Something in Pierre's tone, even under the haze of the fading heroin high, told Death the human didn't really want to go to the hospital. Shaking his head, Death stood and glanced around his flat.

"What? Your accommodations not fancy enough for you? I would think you wouldn't want to go to a hospital or rehab center. They'd ask too many embarrassing questions and expect you to get clean the hard way, cutting off the heroin altogether." Death held up his hand, holding the rest of the drugs. "At least here, you know you'll be getting some more at some point." He glared down at Pierre. "You won't have to worry about me asking questions you don't want to answer. I'm not your psychologist or therapist. I don't really care why you do what you do, whether it's the drugs or selling yourself when you don't have to. There are millions of humans in the world with your exact same story."

Death's chest hurt when Pierre managed to rasp out a harsh chuckle.

"I was always told I wasn't anything special. I guess everyone was right."

Death bit his tongue and turned away while he suppressed the overwhelming urge to deny Pierre's words. He couldn't think Pierre was anything more than a druggie too weak to deal with the world around him.

"Is that what you thought of me?"

"You weren't a druggie. You were simply a boy who made some choices so you could live," Death mumbled under his breath when he walked away from Pierre. "He has the means to live without destroying his soul."

"Really? Just because he has money, his life should be perfect? You were a shining example of how untrue those thoughts can be."

"I don't want to talk to you. I don't understand why you're talking to me now, when I've never heard you in all the centuries since you died."

He stalked into his guest bedroom and made the bed. Pierre would be taking a shower before Death let him touch anything else in his flat. After finishing in the bedroom, he went to the bathroom and hesitated before he started the shower. If he wanted Pierre to clean up, he probably should have done it before the guy shot up.

Shaking his head, he went back into the living room where Pierre sat, hunched over, holding the spoon in one shaking hand and the lighter in the other. Death whirled around and went into his bedroom, stripping his clothes off and throwing them toward the corner. Pierre could just stay in the living room for the night. Death wasn't going to be around while the mortal pushed more poison into his veins.

Standing naked in front of the floor-to-ceiling windows, he stared out at the Eiffel Tower shining, a bright beacon in Paris. The Latin Quarter where Death lived bustled below him, even during the latest hours of night. He smiled, remembering a time when there hadn't been much here, and what had been here were pleasure houses.

After he'd died, it had taken a little bit of maneuvering to get his wealth. He'd managed to get most of it, leaving some for his sister, but he'd kept an eye on her. Emilia had done well for herself. She'd married an English lord and got out of France before the Revolution. At least he hadn't had to escort her soul to the gates for judgment. It had been difficult to do that with some of the others he'd known during his living years. None of them had recognized him, and he thanked the higher powers for that.

"Why were you worried about them knowing who you were? You never liked any of them when you were alive. I remember you lying in bed with me, and how you sneered at the aristocrats, even though you were one of them."

"I was never one of them. I had money but no title, so I was considered less than they were." He thumped his forehead against the cool glass. "Why am I answering the voice in my head? You aren't even real."

"How do you know? Maybe I'm a ghost, and I've loitered around for just the right moment to haunt you?"

"Because ghosts don't exist. No soul lingers in the world after their shell dies. They are always escorted up to the gates." Death closed his eyes. "Besides, if you were real, I would feel even more guilty to know you stayed around for centuries, instead of going to your rest."

The silence in his head startled him, and he wondered what had quieted the voice. Was it that he'd admitted aloud to feeling guilty for what happened to Oliver? He'd admitted it from the moment he'd heard the news, yet he'd never allowed it to cripple him from living the rest of his life.

A soft gasp drifted through his flat, and Death went back to the living room. He ignored the fact he was naked. It wasn't like Pierre would notice either way. Pierre lay flat on the floor, staring at the ceiling, a content smile on his face. Death shook his head in contempt. What could possibly be so bad in this mortal's life he'd turned to drugs to keep the pain at bay? It wasn't like the heroin was a permanent solution to Pierre's troubles. The drug wore off too quickly, and the hunger grew too fast, which was why Pierre needed more and more to achieve his high each time.

Death grabbed a blanket from the back of the couch and laid it over Pierre. He could always wash it afterwards. Death went to the kitchen and searched under the sink. Finally, he found the rubber gloves his housekeeper had thrown in there. After slipping them on, he returned to clean up after Pierre. He discovered a cap for the syringe to cover the needle and put it on. He stuck the spoon, lighter, cotton balls and rubber tubing back into the bag they'd come from.

He placed them on the coffee table before double-checking Pierre was still breathing. Pierre's green eyes caught his gaze, and Death frowned.

"Why do you do this?" Death asked softly. "What demons haunt you to the point where you'd rather inject poison into your veins than face it?"

Pierre didn't say anything, and Death didn't expect him to reply. In the end, it didn't matter one whit why Pierre chose to do this. Death's need to help him stemmed from atoning for something he wasn't even responsible for. He'd sober Pierre up and send him on his way, hoping he would never see him again.

Chapter Three

A thud and a muffled curse brought Pierre out of his stupor just as the heroin high wore off. Need ate at his gut, and he jack-knifed into a sitting position. He moaned softly and scrubbed his hand over his face. *Fuck!* He felt like shit and was pretty sure he smelled like it as well.

After ensuring his head wasn't about to fall off, he glanced around and frowned. Where the hell was he? It definitely wasn't the hotel room he'd been in a couple of days ago. How long had he been out? Long enough for someone to find him and drag his ass somewhere else.

A thought straightened Pierre's spine. Had he been kidnapped? Were the culprits right now trying to figure out how much of a ransom to ask for him? If they were, he wanted to tell them not to bother. No one would pay anything to get him back.

"Are you among the living, finally?"

Pierre jumped and almost fell over onto his side. He braced himself on the edge of the couch and looked up. The man standing a few feet away from him was the oddest, yet most beautiful man he'd ever seen. Pierre figured the man would be about six inches taller than Pierre's own six-foot. His shimmering gray hair was tied back at the nape. Lightly tanned skin attested to the fact the man probably spent most of his time inside, but his muscular build said he also took care of himself. Yet it was the mixture of sadness and coldness in the man's all-black eyes that confused Pierre.

Why did he want to hug the man, and at the same time run away from him as fast as he could? Pierre had never had feelings like that before, and he quite willingly blamed them on the withdrawals snaking their way through his body.

"I'm not sure you'd call what I'm doing living, but I guess I'm still breathing," he muttered.

"Breathing's all some people need to start getting their lives back on track," the man pointed out.

Pierre shrugged. "True, but my train derailed a long time ago. Not sure it's worth the effort getting back on the path of normalcy."

Snorting, the man bent and offered Pierre a hand. "There's no such thing as normal, honey."

He blinked but took the man's hand. Pierre found himself standing upright for the first time in what had to be a week or so. The room whirled around him, and his stomach heaved. God, it would suck if he threw up, since he was pretty sure he hadn't eaten anything in just as long. He leaned into the man and felt him stiffen.

"Sorry. I probably smell like a garbage dump," Pierre apologized before he tried to move away.

"My name is Death, and yes, you do reek to high heavens. There's no way you're going to be able to make it to the bathroom on your own, so I'll deal with the smell."

Death forced him closer again, and Pierre found he didn't have the strength to argue. Not that he wanted to anyway. The warmth radiating off Death called to Pierre at some deep, visceral level. All Pierre really wanted to do was snuggle close and soak up the man's scent and realness.

Yet how did he know the man was real? How did he know anything happening to him was real? It could all be a long-term hallucination brought on by the bad heroin he'd gotten.

"Are you real? What kind of name is Death? Didn't we meet before?" Pierre's tongue ran with all the questions.

As they walked from the living room to the bathroom, Death didn't say anything, and Pierre wondered if it was because he held his breath against the stench rolling off Pierre. If he had the energy, he'd be totally embarrassed, but he couldn't bring himself to be mortified. He'd wait until he could think clearly for that particular emotion.

Pierre propped himself on the counter while Death got the water going. It was only when Death turned to stare at him that Pierre realized he was naked. He glanced down and winced.

"Where'd my clothes go?" he demanded.

"You weren't wearing any when I arrived, and I didn't have time to dress you. I'll bring some of my clothes for you to wear." Death motioned to the steaming bathtub. "Get in whenever you want. I imagine a bath would be easier for you than a shower. Less having to stand, and you're not as likely to hurt yourself from falling."

"Okay." He climbed into the tub cautiously, not wanting to slip or do anything to give Death another reason to be disgusted with him.

He settled in the hot water, cringing at the burning sensation as his skin started turning red. There was a bar of soap and a washcloth on the side of the tub, and he snatched them up. It was amazing that Death hadn't thrown him into the gutter or an alley when he'd found him like the rest of the trash.

Pierre glanced up from his scrubbing while Death returned to the bathroom, holding a few pieces of clothing. He watched as the man set them on the counter next to the sink.

"They'll probably be too big for you, but they'll work for now. Eventually you'll need to call the hotel, have them pack your stuff and send it here." Death started to leave.

"Wait." Pierre bit his lip as Death shot him a glance over his shoulder. Something about the man made Pierre hesitant to ask him any questions. "Where did you find me? Was I wandering the streets or something?"

Death braced his shoulder against the doorframe and tucked his hands in the pockets of his slacks, bringing Pierre's attention to the intriguing bulge under Death's zipper. Swallowing hard, Pierre jerked his gaze away as desire rushed through him. Unfortunately, the drugs kept him from getting a hard-on—or maybe it was a good thing he couldn't show how attracted he was to his rescuer.

No way would a guy like Death want a whoring druggie like Pierre. It didn't matter that Pierre came from a rich family and had somehow managed to make his way through university for a degree. For most people, all they saw were the track marks and the hazy film over Pierre's eyes. They chose to look at the way he flaunted his body for his john. None of them wanted to know anything more about him. They weren't interested in why he sold himself.

"I found you in your hotel room. You were dying from a bad batch of heroin, and I came to take you for judgment." Death didn't seem to notice Pierre's flare of attraction.

"Judgment? Did I get in trouble with the law? To be honest, I don't remember doing anything except going to my hotel room and calling my dealer." Pierre ran the cloth over his arm. "I don't remember leaving or breaking anything to make them call the police on me."

"Not that kind of judgment," Death interrupted him. "I'm Death, the Pale Rider, and I came to escort your soul to the gates to be judged worthy or unworthy."

Pierre laughed and ended up in a coughing fit. Death made no move to help him as he struggled to breathe. When his throat opened and he could fill his lungs, he collapsed against the back of the tub, eyes closed and hands draped over the edges. Pierre concentrated on inhaling and exhaling, hoping his heart would keep beating.

He'd forgotten Death was even in the room until a muffled curse brought his attention back to the man. After opening his eyes, he saw Death had straightened and was standing with his hands clenched, as if he struggled to keep himself from rushing over to Pierre.

"What I was going to say before the coughing fit was I know how that would have ended. I haven't been worthy for anything or anyone for a long time." Pierre fished the cloth out of the hot liquid. He lathered it up with the soap before rubbing it over his chest.

"It's not for you to say whether you are worthy or not. None of us really know how we will be judged in the end." Death pursed his lips and stared at the floor.

Pierre wanted to kiss those lips. Were they as hard as they looked or were they soft and gentle? Shaking his head, he came back to the conversation.

"Aren't you afraid of being judged?" Pierre splashed in the water, enjoying the sensation of being clean.

Death grunted, and Pierre thought that was the only response he was going to get. He was surprised when Death moved over to the toilet and put the top down so he could sit. Pierre didn't mind having someone in the bathroom with him. A few of the johns he'd had liked to watch him clean himself before sex. Something told him Death wasn't like that. Oh, the man might be gay, but he didn't strike Pierre as the type of guy who saw people as objects to be used. Actually, Pierre bet Death didn't really think about people at all.

The gray-haired man struck Pierre as being a loner, wandering through the world without connections or relationships to tie him down. Much like Pierre had been until he'd met Joseph and thought all his dreams were coming true. He should have known better. Dreams were for good people, not for a waste of space like him.

"I must have been judged because I'm doing this instead of spending eternity in Heaven or Hell." Death's vague wave encompassed more than just the room. It seemed to signal the entire world in a way.

"Okay. You said I was dying, and you came to take my soul to be judged. Your name is Death, right?"

Death nodded and rested his elbows on his knees, waiting for Pierre to work it out for himself. There was something familiar about those strange eyes, yet Pierre couldn't remember where he'd seen them before. All he knew it wasn't Death he'd seen.

"Are you saying you're one of the Four Horsemen of the Apocalypse?" Pierre chuckled. "You must have gotten into my stash if you believe that."

Death tilted his head, studying Pierre with an intense expression. "Do I look like someone who would use drugs to dull my life?"

Pierre dropped his gaze to stare intently at the track marks on his left arm. "No."

Of course, there was no way of knowing who needed help to get through the days of their lives. It wasn't like people wore neon signs alerting others to their drug use. Pierre had run across some perfectly normal men and women who were the biggest druggies in the world, but no one would ever know.

He peered through his lashes at Death and accepted the fact that Death definitely didn't have the personality for addiction. No, Death seemed more like the kind of person who bulled his way through life and didn't allow weaknesses to overcome his determination.

"Did you ever love anyone so much you would have done anything for them?" Pierre wanted to slap his hand over his mouth because he'd never meant to ask that question. "Never mind. Don't answer that. I have no right to know."

The glance Death gave him stripped Pierre down to his deepest, darkest soul and left him bare. Pierre didn't know what Death saw there, or even if the man saw anything at all. At times, Pierre thought he was empty inside.

"I've loved one man in my entire existence. I didn't realize how much until it was too late. Maybe if I had been given the option, I would have given my life for him." Death surged to his feet. "Call me when you are finished, and I'll help you out of the tub. I'm going to put some dinner together. I'm sure you're starving by now."

"Yes, sir." Pierre ducked his head.

Well, the conversation had gone as well as could be expected. Pierre still wasn't sure he believed Death about being a Horseman and taking Pierre's soul to judgment. At the moment, it didn't matter. He could function, even with need gnawing at his very marrow.

Pierre finished cleaning off, washed his hair then drained the tub. He didn't bother calling for Death to help him. He was a big enough burden as it was. It wasn't like he hadn't cleaned himself up after binging before, and while it might take him a little longer, he wanted to get dressed without Death glaring at him.

His entire body trembled while he tied the drawstring on the sweat pants Death had left him. Pierre took a step, and it was like Death was clairvoyant. The man appeared just as Pierre's strength gave out and he collapsed to the floor.

"Idiot," Death muttered when he swept Pierre into his arms and carried him out to the dining room. He placed Pierre in a chair, stepped back and stared at him. "Is your brain still messed up? What part of 'call me when you're done' didn't you understand?"

Pierre fiddled with the hem of his T-shirt. "I didn't want to bother you any more than I already have."

Death ghosted his hand over Pierre's wet hair before turning away. "It's too late for that. I'll bring you some food. Oh, and when the need gets to be too much, tell me. I want to see how long you can go before you absolutely need another hit."

"You have more?" Pierre started to surge to his feet, about to go after Death and beg for the stuff.

A quick glance from Death froze Pierre where he crouched, half out of the chair. The cold touch of those black eyes sent a shiver down his spine, and Pierre dropped back into his seat, not willing to risk what might happen if he laid a hand on Death.

"Yes, I do, and no, you can't have it until I'm willing to give it to you. We're going to wean you off the shit before you really do end up killing yourself. You might not think you have anything to live for, but I'm betting there's more out there than you've ever imagined."

Pierre rolled his eyes. "I didn't take you as a pep-talk person."

Death snorted. "Not usually, but maybe I'm getting soft in my old age."

"Dude, you can only be a few years older than me, so that doesn't make you ready for the old folks' home." Pierre fidgeted with the hem of his shirt again.

"You have no idea how old I am, or how many times I've seen people like you destroy themselves for no reason, except life didn't go their way." Death disappeared into what Pierre assumed was the kitchen, given the mouth-watering smells emanating from it.

Pierre glanced around the room. Death wouldn't hide the drugs in obvious places. More than likely he'd hidden them in his bedroom, figuring Pierre would never go in there. Pierre settled into his chair with a smirk. As long as the prize was heroin at the end, he could outwait the man. Death had to leave the apartment at some time, so Pierre would search through his stuff then.

"Here's your dinner."

Death strolled into the dining room carrying a tray filled with steaming food. Pierre's eyes widened at the sight.

"I can't eat all of that," he protested with a shake of his head.

"Eat what you can. I don't think you've eaten for several days. I'm surprised you're even able to move."

Pierre shrugged. "I'm tougher than I look."

Death set the plates in front of Pierre before taking a seat across the table from him. Pierre picked up a fork and glared at his shaking hand. He tried to scoop some of the food up but couldn't get it. His hand shook badly, and it was almost like it wasn't obeying him, no matter how hard he concentrated.

In frustration, he tossed the fork down and fought the urge to scream. Death studied him with a frown.

"I think you might need to be checked out by a doctor. I should have taken you to one when I removed you from the hotel room. You'd already had a bad trip with the tainted heroin."

Before Pierre could protest, Death stood, walked around the table and swept him up in his arms. As much as Pierre wanted to convince Death he didn't need to see a doctor, his energy drained out, and he rested his head on Death's chest.

The dull ache of need presented itself when he wasn't thinking about other things, but he'd felt worse during his rehab time. A thought hit him when Death shouldered his way out onto the roof.

"Why don't you see if the doctor can make house calls? I'll be fine if you have to run out and get him."

He blinked innocently while Death looked down at him.

"I'm not stupid. You think you can find the drugs if I leave, but I want you to know I've hidden it all some place you'll never be able to find it."

Death whistled, and a gray horse materialized out of the shadows. Pierre jerked in surprise.

"I thought I imagined it during my trip, but he did come out of nowhere." Pierre glanced up at Death's chin. "Am I really awake? Maybe this is all a dream and I'm in a coma somewhere."

"It's possible," Death muttered while they approached the horse.

Pierre squeaked when Death set him on top of the stallion, and before he could slide off, Death swung up behind him. Death wrapped his arms around Pierre's waist, pulling him back against Death's broad chest. A bunch of arguments rose in Pierre's throat, but he couldn't find the strength to speak them.

"Where are we going?" Not that he had any way of stopping Death from taking him anywhere.

"We're going to see a doctor. He'll let me know if there's anything seriously wrong with you, and whether I should take you to a hospital."

Pierre didn't have a problem going to a hospital because the moment Death left, he'd check himself out and go to a different hotel. More than likely, he'd call up his dealer and get more shit delivered wherever he ended up.

He gasped when the horse leaped off the edge of the roof, and he stiffened, waiting to plummet to the street. Instead a bright light blinded him, and he lost all feeling in his body. Maybe he had imagined all of it. Maybe he really was dead, and now he would be finding out what was out there after death.

A jolt rocked through Pierre, and a gentle breeze caressed his skin, so they must have arrived at wherever they had been going.

"What the hell are you doing here? I thought we were never going to see each other again. And why am I the one everyone comes to visit?" An accented voice filled his ears.

Pierre groaned while feeling returned to his body and pain rocketed through every nerve ending. He tried to curl into a ball, but something held him in place. Struggling, he fought against his restraints.

"Stay still. We can't have you hurting yourself before we even know what's wrong with you."

It was the strange voice that spoke to him. Pierre swallowed, trying to make his tongue work, or at least get the words he wanted to say out.

"Come on. You have to open your eyes."

The authority in the voice forced Pierre to do as he was ordered. He opened his eyes and stared up into the serious gaze of another handsome man.

"There you go. Now, my name is Aldo, and I'll be examining you. Of course, you have to understand I'm not a practicing medical doctor. I tend to deal with infectious diseases, but my friend here seems to believe I can help you."

"The only real help he needs is to stop being an addict. I just want to make sure nothing's wrong from the overdose he had earlier today. He got some bad drugs, and I need to know if it's messed up his mind or whatever."

Pierre rolled his head to one side. Death stood in the corner, arms folded, a disgruntled expression on his face. Turning back to Aldo, Pierre tried to smile, sure it was probably more like a grimace.

"Where am I now? This doesn't look like a hospital or a rehab center," he pointed out.

Aldo smiled. "You're in Tuscany, where my partner and I have a home. We usually live in America, but we're on vacation. Given the fact I haven't seen Death for several months, I'm surprised he knew where I'd be."

Death grunted. "Just because you're no longer a Horseman, doesn't mean I don't keep track of you."

"Wait a minute."

Another voice joined in, and Pierre managed to tilt his head enough to see a man standing in the doorway, holding a black bag in his hand. The newcomer was blond and younger than Aldo.

"I thought you weren't supposed to have anything to do with the others once they return to be mortals. Also, does he know what you are?" The blond nodded in Pierre's direction.

"Thanks for bringing my bag, Bart." Aldo held out his hand to take the bag.

"Of course he knows what I am. Whether he believes me or not is another story. More than likely, he still thinks this is all brought on by the drugs." Death shrugged. "I don't know and really don't care."

"But isn't it against the rules or something for you to reveal yourself to any mortal?" Bart gestured between Death and Pierre.

"What are they going to do to me? Punish me? Remove me from my position?" Death dropped his gaze to the floor. "They're welcome to do that. It's not like I love my job so much I can't imagine not doing it. Personally, I'd rather find out which gate I'm going to walk through, instead of being stuck in this annoying version of limbo."

"You used to be a Horseman?" Pierre asked Aldo as the man set the bag on the table next to him and opened it.

"Yes. I used to be Pestilence. I figure I can tell you that because Death's already spilled everything." Aldo pulled out a stethoscope and tugged the blanket down from Pierre's chest.

"Shit. When did I get naked again?" Pierre glanced at Aldo and Bart. "Why did I bother to even get dressed?"

He started to yank the sheet back up, but Aldo shook his head. Pierre looked at his hands and saw they were shaking again. He fought to clench them, but he couldn't get them to obey his commands. Looking up, he met Aldo's concerned gaze.

"How long has that been going on?"

"For a couple of months, but it's never been this bad. I've never lost feeling or strength before. Does this have anything to do with the bad shit I got this week?" Pierre bit his lip, not wanting to say anything more. He had the impending feeling of regret.

Why hadn't he just left Paris once he'd realized his lover wasn't going to show? Why hadn't he headed home and called his therapist? Instead, he'd allowed his impulses to take control again and drag him back into the depths of addiction. Why couldn't he be addicted to exercise or shoes? Why did he have to crave something that could kill him?

Aldo examined him without asking any more questions or answering Pierre's. It was like he wanted to check everything out, cover all his bases, before he made any sort of guess as to what was wrong with Pierre.

Chapter Four

Death watched while Aldo examined Pierre. He asked himself why he'd brought Pierre to Aldo. It wasn't just because Aldo was a doctor and it could keep Pierre out of the hospital. Maybe it was because he didn't have any other friends. Even though he lived in one of the busiest cities in the world, Death didn't know anyone there. Not even the tenants in his building.

He'd gotten remotely close to the other three Horsemen. Yet those men were living a mortal life again with their lovers, and he was left behind to continue being the one Horseman all mortals feared. Death had always said their fear didn't bother him. While saying out loud how much he didn't care was easy, it was more difficult for him to admit, even to himself, he did mind.

As Aldo, Bart and Pierre chatted among themselves, Death stared at the tiles under his feet. How many times throughout his life had he been thought of as cold and uncaring? When he was mortal, no one thought he cared about anyone except his sister, and even then he'd never really shown how much he'd loved her.

Well, shooting a man because he'd raped her had to prove the lengths he would go to in protecting her.

Emilia had never questioned her place in his heart. She'd given him trouble and, at times, pushed every button he had. Yet she was the one he'd talked to when he'd learned of Oliver's death. The one who held him as he'd cried that night, yet in the morning, he'd forbidden her to speak of Oliver ever again.

"I still don't understand why you refused to have my name spoken in your presence. No one except Emilia knew who I was."

He refused to answer. No point in making Aldo or Bart think he was crazy. A pair of bare feet came into his vision, and he glanced up to see Bart standing in front of him.

"Aldo wants to talk to Pierre alone, so I'm going to take you to the veranda and pour you some wine." Bart took hold of Death's arm and started to lead him from the room.

Death turned and gazed at Pierre. "Are you okay with this?"

Pierre raised a thin shoulder in a slight shrug. "Do I have much choice? If I'm really in Tuscany, without having a clue how the hell I got here, I can't get back to Paris without money. I'm kind of at your mercy."

"You're not." Aldo glanced at Death, who nodded. "If you truly wanted to leave, we could get you back to Paris, but I think you want to know what's wrong with you before you return."

Pierre rolled his eyes. "Sure. Whatever. You can go have a drink while the doc here plumbs the depths of my neurotic brain."

"If you need me, call out and I'll come get you."

Death allowed Bart to lead him from the room onto the veranda. He took a seat, stretching his legs in front of him. Bart poured him a glass of wine and handed it to him before taking the seat next to him. Death sipped and nodded as the wine danced on his tongue.

"This is good wine, Bart."

Bart waved in the general direction of the grape vines running in straight rows out from the backyard. "They know how to make good wine here. It's a local wine."

He hummed slightly as he sipped again. He let the alcohol soothe him, even though it wouldn't have any real effect on him. Bart didn't say anything at first. They just stayed silent, letting the night sounds ease them.

"Why did you save him, Death? What is it about this man that caused you to break the rules?"

He should have known that Bart wouldn't leave it alone. Death turned the glass in his hand, watching the dark wine slosh from side to side. Should he talk to the man? It wasn't like they considered each other friends or anything. Hell, he hadn't seen either of them since Aldo had become mortal again.

"Pierre reminded me of someone I knew when I was mortal. I couldn't save my friend, but maybe I can save Pierre." Death dipped his head, not wanting to meet Bart's gaze. "I don't want to talk about it."

Bart snorted. "You don't want to talk about it, but I think you need to. Whoever your friend was, he must have meant something more for you to risk getting in trouble with the powers. We don't know what they could do to you for not letting him die and revealing yourself to him."

Death dismissed Bart's worries with a wave. "I have a way to ensure he doesn't remember anything about this entire adventure. The only thing I want for him is to be sober and strong enough to fight his addiction. My friend's death doesn't have any more to do with this than me wanting to be there for someone."

"I didn't get a chance to hang out with you and talk, so there's a lot about you I don't know. Yet I'm pretty sure you've never wanted to be there for anyone, especially after you became a Horseman." Bart poked Death in the arm.

When he looked over at the mortal, he nodded and held out his glass. Bart poured more wine into it.

"You don't know me, Bart, and that's the way I want it. I don't want to be friends with you or Aldo. All I'm asking is Aldo check Pierre out. If there are serious problems, I'll take Pierre to the hospital. The only trouble with that is, Pierre will check himself out as soon as I turn my back, and buy some heroin."

"What makes you think, once you get Pierre clean, he won't just fall off the wagon at the first sign of trouble? It happens, and to be honest, I'm not sure Pierre is interested in getting clean. He strikes me as a man who has a lot of problems."

Death sighed. "Maybe if we give him better coping skills, he'll stay away from the stuff."

"Did your friend die from a drug overdose? Did they have drug overdoses when you were human?"

"Very funny. As long as there have been humans, there have probably been overdoses of some kind or other." Death grimaced. "And no, my friend didn't die of an overdose. He more than likely died of a broken heart."

Death noticed Bart leaning forward to hear the last part as he muttered it. Christ, he really didn't want Bart wondering about Oliver or the reasons why Death was the Pale Rider. He didn't plan on confessing any of his sins to the mortal. Death's life wasn't any of Bart's business.

"A broken heart? There's a story there, I'm sure."

"Not one you're ever going to hear," Death stated when he pushed to his feet. "I'm going to check on Pierre and Aldo. Make sure they aren't getting in trouble with things."

"You'll have to spill your guts at some point, Death. It won't matter who you tell. It's the only way you'll ever be free of being a Horseman," Bart pointed out while he followed Death back into the house.

"What makes you think I want to be free? How do you know I don't love this job?"

Bart burst out laughing. Death glanced back to see the mortal bent in the hallway, arms wrapped around his stomach, laughing hysterically. Death leaned against the wall, his arms folded, and shrugged as Aldo came out to see what the noise was.

"I think your lover finally went over the edge, Aldo. You might want to consider getting him help." Death pushed past the other man into the room.

Pierre sat up on the table, his legs dangling, and his hands braced on either side like he was holding himself up by sheer force of will. His skin was gray under the hint of a light tan, and his auburn hair was soaked with sweat. Pierre bit his lip as he looked up at Death through his eyelashes.

"The need is getting bad, isn't it?" Death guessed while he moved closer.

Pierre lifted his shaking hand to brush some of his hair off his forehead. "I've felt worse."

Aldo snorted when he returned. "I'm sure he has. Okay. I've already told Pierre this, but I figured you probably want to know as well. I couldn't find anything that would have a lasting effect on Pierre from the bad stuff he got. The shaking in his hands and the weakness he's feeling is more than likely from coming down from his last high."

Death nodded, grinding his teeth together while Aldo helped Pierre get dressed. Why did he want to tear Aldo's hands off? Was it because he touched Pierre? Death didn't understand where the possessiveness came from. It wasn't like he planned on seducing Pierre at some point.

He barely suppressed his shudder. No way did he want the skinny man in his bed, not with how he reeked. Even under the freshly showered scent, Death could smell the stench of sweat, fear and death. Pierre was rotting from the inside as the drugs raced through his bloodstream. He didn't think he could look past the lingering aura of self-loathing hanging around Pierre.

"Are you ready to take him back to Paris?"

Death blinked and came back to the room when he met Aldo's gaze. He nodded and reached out to pick Pierre up in his arms.

"I can walk out to wherever you parked your horse," Pierre quipped, obviously willing to overlook the way he couldn't even hold his head up.

"I don't park my horse anywhere. He comes and goes as he pleases," Death mumbled, ignoring the inquisitive glances Aldo and Bart shared.

"Are we going back to Paris? To your place?" Pierre laid his hand on Death's chest, and Death tried to forget how it felt to have someone touch him.

Oliver had done that when they'd lain in each other's arms. He'd rested his hand over the exact same spot and commented on how much he loved feeling the beat of Death's heart. Little had the poor boy known Death didn't have a heart, and he would die cursing the man's name.

"I didn't curse your name when I died. I did call for you, though."

"Thanks for adding to the guilt," Death whispered under his breath when they walked out onto the veranda where Death's horse waited for them.

Pierre rocked his head to the side, giving him a better angle to gaze up at Death. "Who are you talking to?"

"No one, just the voices in my head."

Pierre nodded like he completely understood what Death was talking about. And maybe the man did. No one really knew what happened inside his own head during his trips.

"Sometimes they're the most annoying voices you'll hear all day," Pierre commented. "I'm constantly yelling at mine to shut the fuck up."

"Oh, really? Well, I'll remember that."

Aldo took Pierre from Death so he could mount, but the doctor stopped him.

"What are you going to do with him?"

"I'm taking him back to my place in Paris, then when the hunger gets so bad, he's clawing at his skin to make the pain stop, I'm going to let him have some more. Not as much as his last hit, but not so little his body goes into shock." Death stared at Pierre for a moment before glancing back at Aldo. "His body isn't strong enough for him to quit cold turkey, Aldo. It's not like I want to be his drug dealer."

Aldo frowned. "Where did you get the drugs? I assume heroin is his preferred poison."

There was no way Death would mention Day bringing him the stuff. He didn't want to be involved in the whole convoluted relationship between Day and Lam. He knew Aldo would pitch a fit if he found out Day had any kind of fingers in this problem.

"I know people," he hedged and climbed astride his horse. He held out his arms for Pierre. "Let me have him. He's going to need another hit when we get back.

You're positive there's nothing permanently wrong with him that I should take him to a hospital to deal with?"

Aldo nodded and frowned as he stepped away. "I can't be a hundred percent sure since I don't have any equipment here, but I'd say he should be fine once he's off the drugs."

"I'm going to do my best to get him sober," Death vowed.

"Then what? Are you going to dump him somewhere without anyone to support him? He needs a support system in place to help him when the craving hits." Bart encircled Aldo's waist with his arm and settled beside Aldo like he belonged there.

Which Bart did, Death admitted to himself. Somehow fate or whatever people wanted to call the higher power had done its job and picked the right person for each of the former Horsemen. Death doubted there was a person in the world who would fit him and his wants. Hell, the last time he thought he'd found the right person, he hadn't been there when Oliver had died.

No one had been there when Death had died either, so it was fitting they'd both died alone. Only Oliver didn't deserve to die that way. Death shook his head. He couldn't keep dwelling on those thoughts. It didn't pay to relive his past, especially when he couldn't fix it.

"I'll do my best to make sure he'll have friends who won't lead him astray. Unfortunately, Pierre has money, and that doesn't always lend itself to having friends you can trust."

Death tucked Pierre against his chest and nodded at Aldo.

"Thank you for doing what you could. I'm sorry to have bothered you while you're on vacation."

Aldo hugged Bart closer and smiled. "Anytime, Death. You know I won't turn you away after all you did for us."

Death held up a hand before nudging his stallion with his heels. The stallion snorted but took off in a trot then leaped into the air. A flash of light and Death disappeared into the darkness.

* * * *

Death stared at the man lying on his guest bed. Whimpering, Pierre scratched at his arms. It was time to give the man the next baggie of heroin, but Death didn't want to do it. Maybe he should just let Pierre quit cold turkey. He'd be there to keep an eye on him, and if things were bad, he'd take Pierre to a hospital.

"Man, I'm dying here. Where the fuck is the stuff? You fucking promised you'd give it to me when I needed it. Well, I sure as fuck need it now," Pierre snapped.

It seemed Pierre lost all his politeness when he was going through withdrawals. Death managed to hide his smile as he crossed the hallway and went into his bedroom. He pulled out a small wooden box, unlocked it, and retrieved the next baggie, plus all the paraphernalia Pierre would need to shoot up. He locked the box, returning it to the back of his dresser. It wasn't the ideal hiding spot if Pierre were capable of wandering around the apartment, but at the moment, it worked. When Pierre became more lucid, Death would consider moving it somewhere less obvious.

"Here." He strolled in and tossed the stuff on the blanket next to Pierre. "It's your next hit. It won't be as much, so the high won't last as long, but we'll make sure you go a little longer on the other side of the high."

Pierre lunged for the bags like a cobra after a mouse. Death shook his head and left before Pierre could get anything opened. He wasn't going to sit around and watch the man shoot up.

After going to his study, he sat at his desk and fired up his laptop. Unlike the other Horsemen, he embraced modern times and conveniences. Why not? There weren't any rules stating they had to remain in the dark ages when it came to their living arrangements. He never really understood why Aldo, Baqir and Kibwe had chosen to live apart from mortals.

Death hardly mingled with people, but he didn't totally cut himself off from them and the marvelous modern inventions they'd created. His home screen popped up, and he clicked on his web browser. It was time to do some research on his guest. Death needed to see if anyone was looking for Pierre and if anyone was, whether it was someone Death needed to hide the man from.

He didn't know Pierre's last name, but he did a search of Paris newspapers and found several articles pertaining to the disappearance of hotel heir Pierre Fortescue from his hotel room two days ago. Death frowned. How had they determined Death took him two days ago? Impressive, considering no one had checked on Pierre for several days before Death came for him, or at least, that was what Pierre seemed to believe.

Pierre's stepfather, Jameson Robertson, was offering a reward for any information on the whereabouts of his stepson. Death snorted softly and rolled his eyes. If the man had been so concerned, maybe he should have done more to ensure Pierre stayed off the drugs. Death read more articles and scanned several pages of images of Pierre at all the jet-set hot-spots around the world.

He noticed the same older blond man in many of the pictures. In some, it seemed like Pierre and he were together. In others, the man stood with his arm around a woman while Pierre gazed on with longing in his eyes. Pierre wore his heart on his sleeve about the man, yet Death had a feeling the older man was simply playing Pierre, probably using him for his money and connections.

He found an announcement for the wedding of Lars Holden and some woman set for a week or two earlier. Could this be the catalyst for Pierre's drug binge? It certainly looked like Pierre hadn't been expecting Lars to marry a woman and leave him high and dry in Paris, the city for lovers.

Death shook his head and closed the browser. After standing, he wandered over to the windows and stared out at the Paris skyline. The sun peeked over the buildings, flooding the streets with early morning sunshine. Death smiled, remembering how he'd loved to ride in the parks as the fog burned off the grass. So many sunrises met in such a manner, and he'd never realized how much he'd taken them for granted until he couldn't do it anymore.

Well, he had ridden for a while after becoming the Pale Rider, but slowly, as more buildings had been built and there'd been fewer parks to ride in, he'd stopped. He'd watched as the France he knew tore itself apart during the Revolution, and so many of his peers had ended up being escorted to the gates. He'd never stuck around to find out where they were being sentenced to, because he knew where he'd send them.

"You judge them so harshly, simply because you were never one of them. If you had grown up with money and a title, you would have been just like them."

Death shook his head. No, he didn't believe that. He'd never understood the inherent belief that those in the upper levels of society had in their own supremacy over those less fortunate than them. He'd seen it while living in India and China before he'd come home to launch Emilia into society. The ones with money always seemed to believe God meant for them to have it, and there had to be something wrong with those who didn't have any or they'd be rich as well.

"Yet not all rich people were terrible human beings. Some of them were nice, like the man your sister married. He loved her, even though she wasn't a virgin."

"He loved her money," Death muttered, not wanting to admit Oliver's voice was right.

"Shame on you, Gatian. You know he loved her, or you would never have let her marry him, even if it meant breaking the rules and contacting her to inform her you didn't approve."

"She would have freaked out," Death pointed out. "Considering I was supposed to be dead. I've always wondered if they found my body or if I was pulled through whatever wormhole the Horsemen come through, body and all."

The silence in his head told him Oliver had nothing to say. The feeling of being watched made him turn, and he spotted Pierre propped up in the doorway. The glazed eyes and vague smile told him Pierre had managed to shoot up.

Pierre grinned at him. "Wow, man. You managed to score some top-notch shit. It must have cost you a good penny."

Somehow Death doubted Day had paid for the stuff. He didn't say anything, though. He stood in front of the window and watched as Pierre staggered his way across the floor to hit his knees in front of Death.

"I know I have to pay you for this stuff, but unfortunately, I can't find my wallet or my credit cards. So I guess I'll pay you back the old-fashioned way."

What was Pierre talking about? Death hadn't said a word about any kind of payment. Hell, he didn't want any money exchanging hands, or he really would feel like Pierre's dealer. Pierre reached up and fumbled with Death's belt buckle, trying to get it open.

"Wow…hold on there, Pierre. You're not paying me back that way. I don't want sex from you."

He caught Pierre's wrists in his hands and shoved Pierre away from him. Pierre sprawled on the floor, making his bottom lip plump out in a tempting pout. Death clenched his hands, not giving in to the urge to grab Pierre from the floor and kiss the man within an inch of his life.

Using the shower and changing out of his sweaty clothes had helped Pierre regain some of his good looks, but it didn't take care of the underlying smell of decay. Death wasn't sure he could overlook the scent. He dealt with death every minute of his life—he didn't want his lover to be dying inside while he fucked him.

"Don't you think I'm attractive?" Pierre fluttered his eyelashes before dropping his gaze to look at the bulge growing in the front of Death's pants. "Ah, but I think you do want to fuck me."

Death jerked out of the way as Pierre reached for him again. "Wanting to fuck you doesn't mean I will fuck you. I can control myself, and I don't think you should be whoring yourself out for drugs."

Pierre rocked back on his heels like Death had punched him in the face. Tears flooded his eyes, and he dropped into a ball. Sighing, Death crouched just out of reach of Pierre's grasping hands. He didn't want the man to get a hold of him because it had been a few months since Death had had sex, which was a long time for him. Maybe once he got Pierre settled, he'd go out and look for a quick fuck. It would ease the lust he felt for the mortal currently sobbing on his floor.

"Stop it. I know you're high, and probably have no control over yourself, but at least try to have some dignity. Don't sell yourself so cheap. Being given drugs isn't a good reason to sleep with someone." Death wanted to bite his tongue off.

"Who the fuck are you? My therapist?" Pierre glared at him. "I can fucking do whatever I want with my body. You don't own it. I do."

"I think the heroin owns it, actually," Death commented while he dodged the wild punch Pierre threw at him.

"Fuck you, asshole." Pierre fought to his feet and stumbled out of the door into the hallway.

Death winced when he heard a crash as Pierre ran into something. Pierre didn't seem to take rejection well. Not much he could do about that, though. Death wasn't about to compromise his own morals by fucking Pierre while the man was high. It had taken centuries for Death to develop ethics of some sort—he didn't want to toss them out of the window at the first challenge.

Another crash, and this time it sounded like glass broke as well. Death straightened and headed out to the living room. He had to keep an eye on Pierre to ensure the man didn't hurt himself too badly.

Chapter Five

Pierre stared up at the ceiling of his prison. It had been the third or fourth day since Death had kidnapped him from his hotel room and moved him here. It was Death's apartment, and Pierre assumed they were still in Paris, but other than that, he hadn't been allowed to leave since they'd gotten back from visiting that doctor.

He was coming down from his high, but he had gone longer the last time before he hadn't been able to take it anymore and Death had given him another baggie full of heroin. *Shit!* Could this process be the right way to help him get clean? Weaning him from the stuff a little at a time instead of trying to cut himself off without warning?

A knock sounded on his door, and he rolled onto his side while he called out for Death to come in. Pierre watched as the gray-haired man pushed open the door with his shoulder, carrying a tray of steaming food. Pierre's mouth watered, and he realized he was eating more than he had been before. He could feel his body growing stronger. Maybe this time he would beat this addiction.

Pierre wasn't stupid enough to believe he'd stop craving the drug. *Once an addict, always an addict.* Yet he was smart enough to understand if he was given the right tools, he could find other ways to fight the need, and Death gave him options. Well, options that didn't involve leaving the apartment.

"Here's dinner. I hope you enjoy it."

Death held the tray while Pierre pushed himself up to lean on the pillows. He watched while the man set the tray over his lap, and grinned at the heaped plateful threatening to take over the entire bed.

"I'm not sure I can eat all this," Pierre joked when he picked up his fork.

"Just do your best. Cutting back on the heroin has helped you regain your appetite. You've put on a few pounds so far." Death propped his hip against the dresser while watching Pierre eat. "I meant to bring this up earlier, but I think you might want to call your mother or stepfather. Seems he's started a big search for you. He thinks someone kidnapped you."

"Well, you did kind of kidnap me." Pierre waved his fork around, almost tossing the bite of chicken across the room. "Have you sent a ransom demand? I don't think he'd pay it."

Death tilted his head, studying Pierre with those strange black eyes of his. "What makes you think he won't pay for you? He looked really torn up on the TV when they interviewed him. Your mother hasn't been able to leave the house since they discovered you were gone."

Pierre frowned. Those descriptions didn't sound like the parents he knew. They'd ignored him since he'd turned sixteen. "I'm not sure who you're talking about. My parents never seemed interested in what I was doing."

"You might be surprised by how your family feels, even if they never say it." Death paused a second then continued, "I didn't send a ransom. I don't want anyone's money. Hell, I have enough of my own, and I'm adding more to it every day. How old are you? Aren't you a little old to be rebelling against your parents?"

A laugh burst from Pierre's mouth, causing him to choke on his food. He waved Death away when Death moved to pound on his back.

"Isn't it a little late to ask? I'm twenty-five, not that it matters."

"I didn't think you were a minor, considering how often your picture appears in the tabloids, especially once you'd hooked up with Holden. Figured if you were underage he'd been nailed as a pedophile."

Pierre stiffened at the mention of Lars. He didn't want to think about his ex-lover and how he'd ended up with his heart broken.

"You were in love with him," Death remarked.

He kept his gaze focused on his dinner. "In love with Lars? Hell no. He was just a casual fuck. Didn't mean anything. He got married a week or two ago, didn't he?"

Death strolled across the room and sat on the bed, resting his knee next to Pierre's hip, his hand on Pierre's arm for a moment.

"You know very well he did. I think your binge coincided with Holden's marriage. I think the bastard led you on because you gave him access to your stepfather's money. I did a little research on your on-again, off-again lover."

Pierre didn't want to hear what Death had found out. He'd gone into his affair with Lars with blinders over his eyes and heart. All the warnings from his friends about Lars breaking his heart had bounced right off him because he'd wanted Lars to be his hero, to be the man he could spend the rest of his life with. He should have known it wouldn't work out.

Death fidgeted with the blanket, surprising Pierre, who thought the man would never get nervous about anything. He looked up to see Death staring across the room with an expression on his face like he was listening to something else.

"So will you call your mother? If you want, I'll even let you go home. I don't know what I was doing, thinking I could help you kick this habit of yours. The only way it'll work is if you want to stop getting high, and I'm not sure you want that."

Fear shot through Pierre. As much as being here annoyed him, he didn't want to go out into the world on his own yet. He wanted to hide out and lick his wounds a few days more. So he didn't get as much drugs as he wanted to numb his hurt. At least he didn't have to worry about Death using him for money or sex.

The no sex thing confused Pierre, since he was used to letting men fuck him in exchange for sleeping in their beds and crashing at their houses. Twice Death had refused blow jobs from Pierre, and Pierre wondered what was wrong with the man.

"Are you not gay?"

Death shot a glance at him. "What does that have to do with you calling your mother?"

Pierre shrugged. "Nothing. I just got thinking about something."

"Sex?" Death raised his eyebrows.

"Yeah. I mean, I'm not ugly. In fact, I've been called handsome, gorgeous, or cute all my life. What is it about me that you don't find attractive?"

Okay. The question hadn't come out right. In fact, it had come out rather whiny or childish. He didn't need reassurance of his looks from a stranger. Yet as silly as it sounded, he did want to hear Death say he wasn't ugly, or that Death was attracted to him. How pathetic did that make Pierre?

Death sighed and shifted on the bed like he didn't know exactly what he should say. Pierre didn't want Death to lie to him. He wanted and needed the truth.

"Please, tell me the truth. Don't say what you think I want to hear. I've had too many people kiss my ass over the years. It'd be nice to hear from someone who didn't want something from me." Pierre stabbed at the chicken on his plate.

"Don't worry. You have nothing I need or want. At least money-wise or influence-wise. Trust me, I don't run in the world you do. I have no place there except to take the ones who die up to the gates for judgment." Death turned to meet Pierre's gaze.

"I'm still not clear on what you do. You said you were the Pale Rider. Are you really one of the Four Horsemen of the Apocalypse? I didn't even think you were real."

"We're not supposed to let the mortal world know we exist. I've broken a lot of rules helping you. I'm still waiting to see how it'll all play out. But to answer your question, yes, I'm the leader of the Four Horsemen. Death, who rides the pale horse."

Pierre took a bite and chewed while he thought. He swallowed before he spoke. "Are we in the end times then?"

Death stood and grabbed one of the armchairs placed in front of the fireplace. He pulled it over beside the bed and sat down. After crossing his legs, he steepled his fingers and rested the tips against his lips as he studied Pierre.

Fighting the urge to duck his head, Pierre continued eating. He didn't know what Death searched for, or even if he'd find it in Pierre. No one else had ever found something worth staying for in him. Why would this stranger?

"Some people might consider these to be the end times, but while things aren't particularly good, they aren't as bad as they could be. Though we are known as the Horsemen of the Apocalypse, we are always around. We exist to keep the world in balance." Death focused his attention on the window across the room. He seemed lost in his thoughts for a moment.

Pierre took the time to stare at Death. There was something very old-fashioned about the man, even though he dressed like a *GQ* model in linen pants and a silk button-down shirt. Pierre glanced down at the clothes he wore. Death must have bought them at some point, but Pierre didn't see the man ever wearing them himself. With his gray hair caught at the nape with a leather thong, Death had a rakish air, and Pierre wondered where Death was originally from. The tailored clothes couldn't hide his muscular build, so the man must work out sometime. He was taller than Pierre, and definitely took better care of himself.

"Can you die?" The question popped out of his mouth before he'd even realized he was going to ask it.

Death shrugged. "I'm not sure. I can be injured, but I can't be killed or get sick. I've never been a position where I might die. I think the only person who could end my existence is the one who created me."

"What does being Death mean? Do you touch someone and they keel over dead? How does it work?"

Death chuckled. "If it worked that way you'd be dead by now. I've touched you several times since I found you in your hotel room."

"True. So how does it work?" Pierre set the empty tray on the table next to the bed.

"Pestilence carries diseases and plagues in his hands. His very touch could kill a person in seconds. War has a dagger, and when he stabs someone with it they start battles or wars. Famine wears a medicine bag around his neck filled with salt, and as he travels the world he sows the ground so nothing can grow, causing droughts and famines in his wake." Death held up his hands for Pierre to see. "I follow in their footsteps, picking up souls as they die and taking them to the gates for judgment. My power is simply to extract a soul from its human host, like taking oil from the ground. When a person dies, I touch their forehead and the soul comes out."

Pierre frowned. "Doesn't seem right. You should have a prop like your friends do. Why don't you carry a scythe, or whatever those curved things are? I mean, in all the pictures of Death, he's wearing a hooded cloak and carrying one of those."

"Overly dramatic," Death commented. "I don't need theatrics to do my job."

"Do you ever get tired of it?" Pierre settled back against the pillows and rested his hands on his stomach. "I would think it's pretty depressing, dealing with dead people all day."

"If I really cared, it probably would be, but I don't. They're dead, and nothing I can do would change that fact. I do my job and give the other Horsemen their orders. To be honest, I don't usually do individual deaths. I tend to go for the big massacres or events like that. I was here for the Revolution and had to cart so many souls to the gates I lost count."

Something in the tone of Death's voice told Pierre the Revolution bothered Death more than he'd like to let on. He realized they'd been speaking French without hesitation since he became coherent enough to speak. French wasn't his birth language, but he spoke it like a Parisian.

"Are you French? How long have you been Death? Who were you before you became the Pale Rider?"

Death stood and paced to the other window, hands clasped behind his back. "I am French, and I have been Death for four centuries, since before the Revolution. Who I was isn't important in the grand scheme of things because I'm not the same person I was before I was killed."

"You were killed? How did that happen? Why did someone kill you?"

Pierre was intrigued. What had Death done to end up being murdered? He found his curiosity growing about the mysterious man who'd saved him from an overdose. If Death didn't care about the souls he retrieved, why was he going to such lengths to get Pierre clean and help him kick his addiction?

Death whirled around, and Pierre caught the phone he tossed at him.

"Call your mother. Tell her you're fine, and if you want to go home to her, I'll let you know where they can come to pick you up. I have some work to do."

Smiling slightly, Pierre watched Death stalk from the room. There was a story there, and Pierre was going to have fun digging it out of Death. After the door shut behind Death, Pierre stared down at the phone for a moment.

Did he want to go home? He didn't believe his parents were worried about him. They'd never shown any concern for him when he'd gone on trips and didn't contact them for weeks. Why would they worry about him now?

Yet Death was right. He needed to call and let them know he was okay. He didn't want them to get carried away and call out the army or something. Pierre imagined the security company his stepfather hired to keep track of him had been fired, since Pierre had lost his bodyguard shortly after landing in Paris.

Pierre cringed. The poor guy had probably lost his job, and Pierre felt bad about that. It wasn't the guy's fault Pierre had lost his shit when he'd heard about Lars' marriage. He'd have to talk to Jameson about getting the man hired back on.

Taking a deep breath, he dialed his mother's cell phone number and waited for the hysterics to begin.

"Hello?" His mother's voice held caution. He remembered he wasn't calling her from his own phone.

"Hey, Mom, it's Pierre."

Pierre held the phone away from his ear as she screamed. She sobbed, and he couldn't get her to talk to him.

"Mom, is Jameson there?"

"Yes," she gasped out.

"Then give the phone to him and go get a drink."

Rustling in his ear told him his mother was doing as he told her. He waited for Jameson to start yelling at him. They didn't talk to each other. Mostly Jameson yelled at him for being a selfish, spoiled brat, and Pierre tuned him out.

"Maybe you should listen to him this time. He might not be as bad as you think." Death's voice invaded his mind. Why wasn't Pierre surprised he'd hear Death talking to

him in his head? Yet what Death said was true. Maybe it was time for Pierre to grow up and accept his actions affected other people besides himself.

If Death hadn't decided to help him, he'd be dead, and he'd never get a chance to tell his mother how much he loved her, or thank Jameson for everything he'd done, even when Pierre was being a pain in the ass. Pierre was so surprised by those thoughts, he didn't hear Jameson speak right away.

"Pierre, are you all right? Pierre, come on, you can't scare your mother like that and then not talk to me."

Was that a hitch in Jameson's voice? Could Death have been right about his parents being concerned about him?

"Sorry, sir. I was just choked up at hearing Mom's voice. I'm sorry I haven't called sooner."

"Are you okay? No one's holding you hostage or anything?"

Pierre shook his head before remembering Jameson couldn't see him. "No, sir. I'm fine, sort of. Just completely lost my mind there for a while. I'm really sorry I worried you all."

Jameson swore softly. "When I get a hold of you, Pierre, I'm going to shake some sense into you. Then I'm going to give you a huge hug. Thank God you're okay. Your mother has been out of her mind with worry. We thought for sure someone had taken you."

Pierre swallowed the lump in his throat. "Were you really worried? You never worried before when I left for weeks on end."

"Because your picture always popped up in some tabloid or entertainment show. We knew where you were. This time, once you ditched your security detail at the airport, we had no idea where you went." Jameson cleared his throat. "I fired them, by the way."

"Oh no. Please, hire them back. It's my fault, and they shouldn't be punished for shit I did. I promise, once I get back, I won't try to get rid of them." Pierre closed his eyes and took another deep breath. "I'm sorry, Jameson. Just some shit happened, and I wanted to get away from everything for a while."

"Did you get high, Pierre? Are you using again?"

The disappointment in Jameson's voice hit Pierre hard. Anger swelled in him at the way his stepfather judged him. So much for caring and being worried about him.

"You don't understand what I'm feeling, Jameson." He gripped the phone tight, fighting the need to throw it across the room.

"I saw the pictures of Holden's wedding, Pierre. I know how much you cared for him, but I warned you he was just using you for your money. You didn't listen to me. I'm sorry you got hurt, but if you'd listened to me, this wouldn't have happened."

Pierre shot out of bed and paced the room, ignoring the twinges of muscles he hadn't used in a while. The overwhelming feeling of not being good enough swamped him. It was a feeling he was used to, ever since his mother had married Jameson Robertson. Nothing he did was ever good enough for Jameson, and Pierre never understood why he tried. His real father hadn't wanted anything to do with him either.

"I'm sorry I'm not as goddamned perfect as you are, Jameson. Guess I'm not as smart either, or I would have known from the start what kind of asshole Lars was. Or maybe I was just hoping someone loved me for who I was, not what I could give them."

"You're so spoiled, Pierre. You don't think before you do things, and then you expect other people to clean up your messes," Jameson yelled.

Pierre could see his stepfather in his mind, face red and hands clenched. It was an image he'd been seeing for most of his life.

"What fucking mess did I leave behind this time? As far as I know, I'm the only casualty of this entire fucked-up situation."

"The room you destroyed at the hotel. I had to pay out a good amount of money to keep them from suing you."

"Suing me? Hell, don't I own the fucking hotel?"

Pierre swung around and froze. Death leaned against the doorframe, hands stuck in his pockets, watching him. Pierre's cheeks heated, and he moved toward the other side of the room. Why was he embarrassed that Death had caught him acting like a brat? Nothing Pierre had done in the time Death rescued him had pointed to him being a responsible adult.

"Not yet. Until you turn thirty, your mother owns the hotel. You can still get arrested for trashing it. Where are you, Pierre? I'll send a car to pick you up, and we'll talk about your actions when you get home."

"I'm not coming home. I have some things I need to take care of before I'm willing to set foot in your house."

"Come home, Pierre," Jameson pleaded. "We'll get you the help you need, and maybe then you'll see what you've been doing."

Pierre shook his head, not ready to deal with any guilt Jameson and his mother would press upon him. "No. I'm not coming home yet. I'll call in a couple days to let Mom know I'm okay. Don't try to find me, Jameson. I can disappear if I have to, and you won't hear from me at all."

He hung up and started to throw the phone, but Death was there to stop him. Death took the phone from him, slipping it in his pocket before taking Pierre in his arms. Pierre shivered at the warmth radiating from the man, and also the security he felt wrapped in Death's embrace. Christ! How messed up did that make him?

The pain and anger swelled and ebbed inside him, and he longed for heroin to chase the emotions away. It was one of the reasons he'd started using to begin with. So many emotions and no way to let them out. He encircled Death's waist, gripping the back of the man's shirt in his fists. Pierre burrowed his face into Death's chest, breathing in the intoxicating and expensive cologne Death wore.

"I need a hit," he whispered.

Death rocked him and ran a hand over Pierre's back. Death's touch soothed Pierre in a different way from the drugs.

"No, you don't. You need to sit and think about what's making you angry. Drugs mask the problems, Pierre. They don't fix them for you. Once you come down from the high, everything you ran from will still be there, waiting for you." Death eased him back and studied him. "Wouldn't it be better to fix the problems instead of running from them? Once you find a solution to them, they'll disappear, and you won't ever have to face them again."

Pierre had heard the same shit from his therapist at the rehab center, yet somehow hearing Death say it made it sound different. He stared up into those black eyes, and something caught hold of him. Pierre slid his hand into Death's hair and dragged the man's head down to bring their lips together.

He expected Death to jerk away from him and berate him for kissing him, but Death did nothing except pull him closer. Their lips rubbed together in soft, gentle kisses. They were different from the kisses Pierre was used to getting from Lars and other men. They demanded he open for them. They invaded his mouth like there wasn't any doubt he'd let them in.

Death teased and licked along the seam of Pierre's mouth, asking for entrance. He didn't demand or force. There was nothing except acceptance. Pierre pushed up on his toes, trying to get as close as he possibly could to Death without slipping under the man's skin.

He gasped when Death grasped his ass and squeezed. Chuckling, Death swept his tongue into Pierre's mouth, and Pierre tasted the whiskey Death had sipped sometime earlier. Death ran his tongue over Pierre's teeth.

Pierre wound his leg around Death's thigh, wishing they were naked and he could feel all of Death's skin against him. His lungs were burning for air when Death broke their kiss. Pierre hid his smile as Death rested his forehead on Pierre's, trying to catch his breath.

"We shouldn't be doing this," Death pointed out.

"Why not? It takes my mind off the drugs." Pierre tugged Death's hair free of its tie and ran his fingers through the silken strands.

Chapter Six

"I don't want to be a substitute for the heroin. I can't become your new addiction, Pierre." Death set Pierre aside and stalked off, not happy with how he'd allowed his lust to take over. He searched his pockets for another hair tie and pulled his hair back into a tail again.

He shot Pierre a glance. The man had his fingers resting on his lips with a stunned expression on his face. Death didn't know if the expression was because Death had denied him or because the kiss was just that awesome.

"You don't want me then?"

Snorting, Death strolled back to Pierre and grabbed his hand. He pressed it against his erection straining against the front of his pants.

"Does it feel like I don't want you?"

Pierre grinned with wicked joy, but Death shook his head.

"Just because I want you doesn't mean I'll take you. You have issues, Pierre. The first of which is your lack of impulse control. Your need to dull the harder emotions for fleeting highs like heroin or sex." Death brushed a lock of hair back from Pierre's face. "Trust me when I say I've been where you are. I didn't use heroin or opium to soften the edges of my pain. I used alcohol, and by drowning my sorrow, I let someone I love down when he needed me most."

"Won't happen to me because no one needs me. I'm expendable, tossed away at the slightest whim." Pierre winked at him. "But that doesn't mean I'm not fun while I'm being used."

Rolling his eyes, Death turned away from Pierre. He headed toward the door but kept an ear out for Pierre. The mortal followed him as he made his way out to the living room. Death dropped onto the couch, resting his elbows on his knees. Pierre chose to curl up in one of the large chairs flanking the couch.

Pierre's skin was pale now with a gray tinge to it, telling Death the need was starting to build inside. Pierre seemed to be going longer and longer without having to shoot up. Maybe Lam and Day's idea of weaning Pierre off the heroin was working, though there was going to come a day when Death didn't have any more heroin to give Pierre. That day would be the beginning of a new life for Pierre, hopefully a clean and sober one.

"How did your phone call go?" He needed to take the conversation back to what was really bothering Pierre.

Pierre shrugged. "It started out okay, but ended like most of them usually do."

"How's that?"

After hearing just the tail end of Pierre's part, Death had a good idea what Pierre meant.

"Jameson telling me what an ungrateful child I am. I've never understood how well I've had it. He always has to come and clean up my messes. How I should have listened to him when he told me Lars was a user." Pierre plucked at the hem of his T-shirt. "Is it too much to ask to for someone to want me for myself? Yet no one ever has. I mean, even my real dad abandoned me with my mom. I shouldn't be surprised."

Death could see Pierre was working himself into a funk. He clapped his hands together and stood. "You should go take a shower and change into some nice clothes. There are some hanging in the closet that'll fit you. We're going out to walk around and maybe grab a very late supper."

Pierre perked up, his eyes shining at the thought of getting out of the apartment. Death would probably end up regretting it, but there wasn't any real reason to keep the man locked up in the apartment. Death was getting restless as well. Lam hadn't come with any orders for him or the other Horsemen lately, and Death wasn't used to just sitting around, waiting for something to happen.

It was time to leave the city and head out to the country. Somehow, he'd had managed to hold onto the family country estate, even after his death and the Revolution. He'd bought it from Emilia, and she'd been glad to see it go, saying it reminded her of him. Of course, he'd gone through a middleman to buy it.

"Go on. Your need isn't very strong right now. Maybe if we distract you, you can go a little longer." He waved toward the bathroom.

Pierre shot out of the chair and raced down the hallway. Smiling, Death tugged out his phone and dialed the caretaker for his country place, letting the man know he would be out there by the end of the week. The place would be stocked with food and drinks, along with whatever else the caretaker thought he'd need. It would be aired out as well by his housekeeper.

He listened to the shower turn on, and moved out on to the balcony, trying to remember the last time he'd had someone in the apartment for an extended period of time. Or the last time he'd taken another person out to the country house. Leaning against the railing and looking out over the Latin Quarter, he realized it had been a very long time since he'd become attached to someone or cared enough to let them into his life.

Oh, he never went long without sex, but Death usually fucked them in a hotel room where he could leave whenever he wanted, and they didn't have to talk at all. No awkward next-morning moments. He didn't do relationships, hadn't done even when he was mortal.

"I do remember spending a night or two in your bed."

"You were the only exception to my rule, and look how that ended," Death spoke out into the darkness.

"But it was nice until the end. I had no complaints."

"None? Wouldn't you have rather I made you my lover and set you up in your own house?" He rubbed his hands together, working to erase the faint memories of how Oliver's skin felt under his fingers.

"Certainly, but I knew the rules when I became a whore. A man like you doesn't get attached to a body he can buy at a pleasure house. Of course, when I chose my life, I wasn't expecting to meet someone like you."

And Death hadn't expected to meet someone like Oliver. He closed his eyes, bringing up an image of his lover. A brilliantly white smile with crooked teeth in a lightly tanned face. Bright, green-gold eyes filled with such admiration for Death it hurt sometimes. Oliver pressing his slender body into Death's, silently begging for him to take him the first time Death had bought him. The sex had been something more than between a patron and a whore. Every time after that was etched into Death's memories, and every encounter afterwards never lived up to those nights in Oliver's arms.

"I'm sorry," he whispered, knowing it was too late for absolution.

It wasn't really Oliver's voice he heard in his head. It was his own mind making up the words he hoped Oliver would say if he were still alive. He'd begged forgiveness at Oliver's graveside many nights in the years following the young whore's death. Yet he'd never felt like Oliver heard him.

"Death? Where are you?"

"Out here."

After turning, he leaned against the rail to watch Pierre walk out on the balcony. The clothes he'd bought for the young man looked good on him. A green silk shirt complimented his eyes, and the tight jeans framed his slender hips and pert ass. He wore black dress shoes.

"Are you ready to go?"

Pierre's eyes glowed with excitement, and Death's breath hitched in his chest. On more than one occasion he'd seen just such a look in Oliver's eyes when Death had walked into the room.

Was this his chance at redemption? Pierre wasn't a whore selling himself on the street, though he had sold himself to men for drugs. It wasn't like Pierre had to do it to survive, but still he had at times in his life. Could Death saving him from killing himself with drugs erase the mark made against Death's soul when Oliver had died? Did it matter all these centuries later?

"Death? Are you ready to go?"

Death smiled at Pierre's eagerness. "Yes. Let's go."

He snatched up his wallet, keys and double-checked to make sure he had his phone before they left. Death also grabbed two jackets, handing one to Pierre as he stepped into the hallway. It was still a little cool in April in Paris. As they waited for the elevator, Pierre could barely hold still. Death shot him an amused glance.

"Why didn't you say something about going out before this?"

Pierre shrugged. "I figured you wouldn't let me because I could get away and track down a dealer."

"You could still ditch me and score yourself some," Death pointed out.

He chuckled at the disbelieving glance Pierre shot him.

"Somehow, I think you'd be able to find me without any trouble, and my ass would be grass if you found out I bought drugs."

Death inclined his head as the elevator arrived. He motioned for Pierre to enter the car first.

"You're right about me finding you, but I'm not your parents, Pierre. I would hope you would be able to resist the temptation. Yet you haven't shown much ability to control yourself. Who knows? Maybe by the time I'm done with you, you'll have grown up a little bit."

Pierre looked like he wanted to argue, but they arrived at the lobby before he could think up something to dispute what Death had said. Death escorted him out of the building and onto the crowded street. Pierre shrunk back into Death at the sound and sights greeting them, but Death simply took Pierre's hand in his and started strolling along with the flow.

He wanted to get Pierre out and work on his cabin fever. Pierre clung to his hand at first, not lifting his head very often.

"Are you afraid someone will recognize you?" he asked after Pierre turned his head away from a random tourist taking a picture.

"Yes. If they get a picture of me with you, wandering around here, it'll get posted online, and Jameson will see it. He'll have this place blanketed with men looking for me." Pierre shrugged. "I don't want to go home yet. I want to kick this habit, but rehab centers don't seem to work for me."

"They didn't work for you because you weren't ready for them. Did your parents force you to go the first two times?" Death eased them around a street performer, dropping money in the man's bucket as they went by.

"Thank you, sir," the man called out and Death waved a hand at him.

Pierre studied the people swirling around them. "Yes. They admitted me both times, telling me they were concerned about my health, and they worried I was killing myself slowly. Really I was just embarrassing them, and they wanted to hide me away for a while until the news moved on to something else."

Death didn't believe Pierre's parents were entirely selfish with their actions. He had the feeling they did worry about Pierre, but the man was stuck in his childish world of believing no one loved him. He moved Pierre's hand to the crook of his elbow, and Pierre didn't object as they wandered.

"Where did this belief no one loves you come from?"

Pierre stopped in the middle of the stream of people to glare at Death. "What makes you think I believe people don't love me? There are a ton of people who love me, and I spend a lot of money to ensure they do."

Death tugged on Pierre's hand, forcing him to move. He wasn't interested in stopping at the moment. There was a particular restaurant he wanted to eat at, and they had reservations there in ten minutes.

"Ah, see, having someone act like they love you because you're paying them isn't the same as them loving you because you're you."

He spoke from experience. Most of the people who'd hung around him when he was mortal did so because of his money, not because they liked him or even knew him, for that matter. Death hadn't cared since they'd barely registered on his radar. They weren't important and never had been, even before Oliver's death. Afterwards, they were more like ghosts flitting in and out of his world and had no effect on him whatsoever.

"How would you know?" Pierre stumbled along beside him. "Were you rich when you were alive?"

"I'm alive now, just in a different way, and yes, I was extremely rich for the time period. Hell, I'm ungodly rich now since I've had centuries to build up my fortune." He smiled and nodded at Pierre's shocked glance. "So yes, I understand what it's like to be surrounded by people who only care about your money, but I think you're doing your parents a disservice by thinking they were only concerned about their image."

"How would you know? Have you talked to them? Are you their therapist as well as mine?" Pierre pouted.

Death rubbed his thumb over Pierre's bottom lip. "No, honey, I haven't talked to them, and I'm not taking their side. In fact, I'm not taking any side to this issue. I was simply stating you should try to see the whole picture instead of your narrow view of it."

"I don't want to talk about them or this whole situation anymore."

"All right. What do you want to talk about?"

Death ignored the stares of strangers as they walked by. He knew how odd he looked with his gray hair and black eyes. Most people assumed he wore contacts, and he wasn't about to dissuade them of that idea. Maybe he should have grabbed his sunglasses, but wearing those at night tended to cause even more curiosity, and he didn't want to make Pierre uncomfortable.

"Do you have a destination in mind or are we just walking along?" Pierre edged a little closer, hugging Death's arm tight for a moment. "It's like we're a couple, and they say springtime in Paris is for lovers."

"Have you never done anything with another man like this? Just spending time together?" Death enquired when they arrived at the restaurant.

Pierre stayed silent while the hostess greeted Death before leading them to a private table in the corner where shadows would hide them from prying eyes. Death took Pierre's jacket and hung it up with his on the hook on the wall beside their table. He held out a chair and waited until Pierre sat before he pushed it slowly up to the table, like any gentleman would do for his date. He took a seat and nodded as the waiter approached with a bottle of wine.

"Would you like a glass?"

Nodding, Pierre stared at him with a puzzled look on his face. The waiter poured a little bit into Death's glass, who made all the right moves before pronouncing the merlot perfect. Like there was any doubt, considering it was his own personal bottle he'd sent over before they'd left the apartment.

The waiter filled both glasses to just the right spot and left after a slight bow. Death waited Pierre out. He knew the man was bursting with questions, but decided he would have to ask them before Death volunteered anything.

"Are you a regular?" It seemed Pierre was going to go with a safe question.

"You could say that." Death smiled at the chef when he headed in their direction. "You could also say I own the restaurant."

The chef greeted Death with a barrage of Portuguese, and Death replied, noting Pierre's surprise. After the chef left, promising to cook Death and his guest the most wonderful dinner ever, Pierre took a sip of his wine and frowned.

"So you speak Portuguese?"

Death chuckled. "Pierre, I've been around for centuries, and while I don't particularly like people, I haven't lived like a hermit either. Unlike my counterparts, I chose to remain in the city of my birth and watch it become the vibrant city it is at the moment."

"Your counterparts? You mean the other Horsemen?" Pierre kept his voice down, obviously understanding he shouldn't be letting anyone overhear their conversation.

Normally Death would stick to the no-talking-about-Horsemen rule, but lately he'd been getting tired of the secrecy. As far as he was concerned, if the powers that be didn't like him discussing the Horsemen with Pierre, they could come and stop the entire relationship. In a way, he hoped they would, because he had grown weary of his whole existence. Maybe that was why he'd chosen to take Pierre and try to sober him, instead of allowing him to die.

"Yes, the other Horsemen, or at least the last round of them. All three that were around when I was chosen to be Death are no longer Horsemen. While they were Riders, they chose to isolate themselves from mortals. I didn't, and I've found I'm better for it, though still isolated in my way."

Pierre took a piece of the freshly baked bread the waiter had brought over, and bit into it. Death could almost see the wheels in his head spinning. Death looked out into the restaurant, judging how well things were going that night by the smiles on the customers' faces. Most of them seemed quite happy with the food.

Their waiter returned with their *hors d'oeuvres*, a very aromatic soup, and Death picked up his spoon to dip in.

"Why are you treating me like we're on a date?"

Ah, now they were getting to the real questions Pierre wanted to ask. Death set his spoon down and picked up his glass, leaning back in his chair to study Pierre.

"Does it matter why I'm treating you like this?" Death motioned to the table. "We're drinking excellent wine, about to eat a marvelous meal, and go for a stroll along the Canal Saint-Martin when we're done."

"What are you going to want from me when we get back to your apartment?" Pierre fidgeted with his silverware.

Death replaced his glass and reached across the table to cover one of Pierre's hands with his. He waited until Pierre looked at him before speaking.

"I don't expect anything, Pierre." He paused for a moment then continued. "I was wrong. I do expect something from you."

Pierre's expression hinted at disappointment. "Should have known you were too good to be true."

Snorting softly, Death shook his head. "It's not what you think. While I do find you attractive, I won't lie about that, I'm not expecting you to sleep with me in exchange for a nice dinner. I have never done that with any of the men I've slept with. This dinner comes with only one expectation, and it's that you enjoy yourself. That's all."

"Yeah, right. You say that now, but when we get home, I'm sure you'll be pointing at the bedroom, ordering me naked on my hands and knees." Pierre stirred his soup furiously.

Shaking his head, Death let go of Pierre's hand and leaned back again, running his fingers around the rim of his wineglass. "I'm not sure who you dated before, but no one should be treated like that."

"Not even a whore?" Pierre flushed, and Death figured he hadn't meant to say that.

"I have bought the favors of a whore many times, especially before I died, and I've never treated them in such a manner. It hurts no one to be nice, even when it is understood there will be sex. It's only right to treat your lover as you would want to be treated."

Grimacing, Pierre glanced around, and Death made a decision. He flagged down their waiter.

"Box all the food up and have it delivered to my apartment."

"Yes, sir." The waiter didn't ask any questions.

He stood and went to Pierre's side. After Pierre stood, Death helped him slide his jacket on before they strolled from the restaurant, heading for the canal. He tried to organize his thoughts, not wanting to say anything that would upset Pierre unintentionally.

Pierre walked beside him, holding his hand, but not saying anything either. He was probably confused by Death's actions, since from what he'd said so far, no man had ever treated him nicely.

"You have to value yourself higher than you do, Pierre."

Death tightened his grip as Pierre tried to pull away from him. He stepped closer to the low stone barrier that kept people from falling into the canal, and leaned against it, tugging Pierre into the space between his legs. Death let go of Pierre's hand to cradle his face. They stared at each other, and Death shook his head.

He brushed his lips over Pierre's. Pierre moaned, but Death didn't take it any deeper. Staying only inches away, he whispered, "You are worth more than you think, and we just have to figure how to make you believe that."

"No one else has ever thought I was worth something," Pierre confessed, his green eyes vulnerable instead of hard.

"Actually, I think there are a few who think that, but you're so caught up in the louder voices, you can't hear the quiet ones." Death caressed Pierre's face, trailing his thumbs over the man's cheekbones.

Pierre was looking better, though Death could tell the need was starting to gnaw at him again. He'd gone far longer this time than ever before, and after this last hit, there would be no more heroin, which was another reason why Death wanted to leave Paris. It would be harder for Pierre to find a dealer out in the country.

There was a brighter gleam in Pierre's eyes, and his skin didn't have the underlying gray pallor to it anymore. There was still a faint hint of decay in his scent, but Death knew it would fade once the drugs were completely out of his system.

"Why do you care?"

It was the question Pierre had been struggling with since the entire situation had started, Death knew, and he finally might be ready to believe the answer.

"Because there was a man I loved very much, but I was too scared or too full of pride to admit how much he meant to me, and I lost him." Death looked over Pierre's shoulder for a moment, not seeing the people walking by. He was lost in the past, remembering a night much like this when he and Oliver had wandered down a street.

"What happened? Did he get tired of waiting and fall in love with someone else?" Pierre asked, his question shattering Death's memories into a million sharp pieces.

"No. He died, and I was drunk in another man's bed when it happened. If I had been with him like I was supposed to be, he wouldn't have died."

Death wanted to turn away from Pierre. Having the man stare at him was cutting into what was left of his soul. Yet he didn't see any pity or accusation in Pierre's gaze. There was a strange look, almost like understanding on Pierre's face.

"I've been there. Drunk in another man's bed when you were supposed to be with someone else. Of course, my mistake didn't end with the other person's death, but still, how were you to know he would die that night?"

Pierre was absolving him of Oliver's death, but Death knew the truth. If he'd been there, Oliver would never have taken his killer to his bed because Death would have paid for the entire night with him. Instead, Death had allowed a stranger to seduce him and convince him to go to his bed, and Oliver had died at the hands of another man.

Death changed the subject. "I thought we'd go to the country tomorrow. I have a house a couple of hours away, and I think it might be good for you to leave Paris for a while. Also, in case someone has spotted you, they won't know where you've gone from here."

"No one knows who you are?"

They turned to head back to the apartment building. Death tucked Pierre's hand in the crook of his elbow once again, only this time, it felt like they really were a couple, strolling along during a cool Parisian night.

"I've hidden my identity behind several aliases. Trust me, your parents won't find us if you don't want them to. They can't even track my phone number." Death glanced over at Pierre. "You're as off the grid as you can be without living on the streets. Also, you're not as strung out on drugs as you could be. Hopefully, by the time you decide to resurface and go home, you'll be clean."

"Are you sure you want to be stuck with me out in the country? At least here, you could leave and visit museums or something if I got too obnoxious."

Death laughed loudly. "Honey, do I look like someone who would go to museums?"

Pierre studied him for a moment before shaking his head. "No, not really. You're more the type of guy who goes out and does some sort of physical activity."

"True. I have horses at my country estate. Do you ride?"

"Not as well as I ride other things." Pierre winked.

"You're shameless." Death smiled. "Come along. We need to get some sleep. I want to leave early in the morning."

"Yes, sir."

They remained silent the rest of the way to their place. After locking the door behind them, Death hung up their jackets before looking at Pierre. The man stood in the middle of the living room, absently scratching his arm. Death leaned against the back of the couch, trying to decide if he should offer the last of the heroin.

"Are you okay?"

Pierre glanced over at him, then down at his arm. He clenched his hands before shaking his head. "No, I'm fine. To be honest, the symptoms aren't so bad now.

You were probably right to wean me off like this instead of forcing me to go cold."

"I have one more baggie of heroin, Pierre. Aside from wanting to get you out in fresh air, and maybe spend some time alone with you, I wanted you out of the city so you're not tempted to steal away and score some more."

Scowling, Pierre stared at his feet for a moment. "I'm glad you added you wanted to spend time with me. Doesn't sound quite as much like you're babysitting me. You're right to worry about me sneaking out. If I'm bored, I could end up doing that without even really needing to score."

Death watched Pierre sigh and turn to head down the hallway.

"Keep the last bag. I've gone this long without it, and the withdrawals aren't bad. I can handle them so far. Who knows? Maybe I won't ever need that last hit."

Death sincerely hoped Pierre was right, but he wouldn't hold his breath. They would be able to breathe easier after a few months of Pierre being clean. He wandered to his room and packed before climbing into bed and falling asleep with Oliver's image merging with Pierre's.

Chapter Seven

The chauffeur drove the car smoothly up the sweeping driveway, and Death watched his house grow bigger while they got closer. They could have traveled using Death's horse, but he thought Pierre might like a more conventional mode of transportation. The way Pierre's eyes had lit up when the classic Rolls-Royce had pulled up to the curb told Death his choice was the right one.

"This is your place?" Pierre peered out of the window when they approached the house.

"Yes. Why do you sound so surprised? I'm sure you've been in places far bigger than mine, and hung out with people far richer than me," Death pointed out.

"Sure, but most of those places belonged to other family members. The people I hung out with didn't own them. I'm guessing you've owned this for a long time." Pierre shot him a quick glance.

Death nodded. "It's been in my family for centuries."

He couldn't say any more than that with the chauffeur up front. He didn't have a problem with telling Pierre the truth, but he wouldn't risk something happening to his driver. Death looked at Pierre and sighed silently. He knew what he'd have to do once Pierre was ready to leave, and he didn't like the idea of Pierre not knowing Death was in the world. Yet he had a feeling if he didn't do it, Lam would come and wipe Pierre's memory.

Maybe he should do it right now and return Pierre to his parents, but selfishly, Death wanted more time with the man before he became nothing more than a faintly thought of dream.

The driver rolled the car to a stop in front of the sweeping stone staircase leading up to the oversized wooden doors. Johnson, the man Death left in charge of the estate when he was in the city, stood at the top of the stairs. Death smirked at the stereotypical image of a butler the man presented.

"Who's that?" Pierre whispered as they climbed out of the car.

"That's Johnson. He's my right-hand man here at the estate. If you need something we don't have, tell him, and he'll get it for you." He held up his hand to keep Pierre from saying anything. "Except heroin. He won't be your dealer either."

Pierre wrinkled his nose but didn't complain or protest. They climbed the stairs, and Death shook Johnson's hand.

"It's nice to have you back, sir. I'm sure you'll find everything is in order." Johnson bowed slightly.

"Thanks, Johnson. This is Pierre. He'll be my guest, and if he needs anything, please get it for him, unless he asks for drugs. Those aren't on the menu here."

"Yes, sir." Johnson faced Pierre. "Welcome to Almasia Estates, Master Pierre. I'm sure you'll be happy here."

There wasn't a flicker of disgust or disdain in Johnson's face because of Pierre's status as a drug user. It was one of the reasons why Death liked Johnson. The man didn't judge people on what they were. He judged them on their actions, and as long as Pierre treated Johnson with respect, Johnson would do the same.

"Thank you, Johnson." Pierre offered his hand for Johnson to shake.

They shook as Death pushed the doors open and stepped into the foyer. It had been several months since he'd last been there. He'd spent Christmas in Paris, not wanting to deal with the memories going to the estate would have brought on. Pierre and Johnson followed.

The chauffeur put their bags just inside the door, where the footmen would carry them upstairs. Johnson dismissed him with a soft order.

"I took the liberty of putting Master Pierre in the Gold Room next to your suite," Johnson said as Death stripped off his coat.

Death paused for a second before continuing like nothing was wrong. Could he deal with someone else being in that room? No one had used it since the fortnight Oliver had spent with him the Christmas before Oliver had died.

"It's time to let go, Gatian. I'm not going to come back, not even as a ghost."

Maybe not a ghost, but apparently Oliver's voice was going to haunt Death for a while. He grimaced before nodding at Johnson.

"Yes, the Gold Room will be fine."

Johnson gestured toward the back of the house. "A light breakfast has been laid out in the Red Breakfast room, if you would like."

Death placed his hand at the small of Pierre's back, gently urging him to walk down the hallway. "My cook is marvelous, and I wouldn't pass up anything she made."

Pierre choked back a laugh.

Leaning over, Death whispered in Pierre's ear, "We don't stand on ceremony here, no matter what it might seem like. I want you to feel comfortable here, Pierre. So laugh, shout, and make as much noise as you want. Sometimes I think the silence can get too heavy."

"Do people know what a gentle soul you have?" Pierre turned to look at him, and their lips brushed.

Death inhaled and stepped back. He was getting too close, and Pierre was seeing what Death had managed to keep hidden for centuries. Was it time to push Pierre away? Yet the lonely part of Death's heart didn't want the man to leave. He wanted Pierre to stay for a while longer.

"No. I've managed to fool them all into thinking I'm a hard ass." He winked, diffusing the emotional moment.

"Well, you do a good job of that as well." Pierre slid into the chair Death held for him.

"It's easier than letting people think they can walk all over you."

Death took a seat and his footman served them breakfast. He smiled at the expression of being slightly overwhelmed on Pierre's face. After the man poured the coffee and left, Death laughed aloud.

"Isn't this all a bit much? Do they do this all the time?" Pierre waved a hand toward the table and plates.

"The first day I'm back, they do this. Tomorrow, we'll be serving ourselves, and you won't have to worry about anyone asking you if you need help getting dressed. Johnson just likes to show me the staff still knows how to serve properly."

Death picked up his fork and took a bite of the waffles his cook had made. He practically moaned as they melted on his tongue. Soon the only sounds filling the room were the clink of silverware against china, and the moans as they ate the exquisitely prepared food. Finally, Death pushed his empty plate away and leaned back, holding his coffee cup. He watched Pierre almost lick his plate clean, smiling as Pierre stretched and yawned.

"Are you ready to take a nap? We did get up rather early this morning. The tour of the grounds can wait until after lunch. Why don't I show you to your room? You can rest, plus there's a TV and a computer in your suite." Death stood and motioned for Pierre to join him.

"What are you going to do?" Pierre peered into the rooms they passed on their way back to the foyer.

"I'll be working most of the morning, so I can spend the afternoon riding around my estate."

Pierre stopped and gazed at the ceiling in the foyer. It was a beautiful reproduction of the Sistine Chapel in Rome. After Death had returned to France at the end of World War Two, he'd hired an artist to do it for him. It wasn't nearly as perfect as the original, but no one stood very close to it, and he was satisfied with it.

"Is this the same house you owned when you were alive?" Pierre's question was low as they climbed the stairs.

"Yes. I kept a hold of it. I'm surprised those in charge let me do as much as I did. I had been warned about not letting mortals know we existed yet I never let anyone know what I was. They all assumed I was some eccentric rich man. Of course, if I'd been poor, they'd have thought I was crazy." He rolled his eyes.

"Is your apartment building the house you used to own when you were mortal?"

Death led the way down the left hallway, trying to figure out if Pierre needed to know the truth, or if it really mattered any more. He stopped in front of the Gold Room, and clasped the doorknob in a white-knuckled grip. Something about his silence must have alerted Pierre to his struggle.

"You don't have to tell me. I'm just curious. You know, you're the most interesting person I've met in a long time, and not just because you're a Horseman. Not that I'm entirely sure what they are."

Death pushed open the door and stepped to the side when Pierre walked past. He breathed in Pierre's scent, and the familiar cologne of mint drifted by his nose.

"The building used to be a pleasure house, or a whore house as you might know them. It was where the man I loved worked."

His mouth open in surprise, Pierre blinked at him, and Death realized he'd said too much.

"I'll leave you to your rest."

After shutting the door behind him, he moved to the next set of doors and went into his room. He shut and locked them before stripping and putting on a pair of worn jeans and a long-sleeved shirt. Death dropped to the edge of his bed and scrubbed his hands over his face.

Where the hell had that scent come from? Death wasn't even sure the cologne Oliver used to wear was still being manufactured, or was Death's mind playing tricks on him, making him see similarities that weren't there?

He fell back on the bed, staring at the ceiling. This mural depicted the Four Horsemen of the Apocalypse as they burst from the seals. It was awe-inspiring and kind of scary, yet Death got an odd sense of security from it, knowing there were three others out there, going through the same shit he was.

"But they aren't the same ones you knew the best."

"I wondered when you'd show up again," he said, rolling his head toward the end of the bed where Lam stood. "What took you so long?"

The angel strolled over to the French doors leading out to a balcony. He didn't open the doors, just pulled back one of the curtains. "You're not the only one I keep an eye on."

"You have a whole herd of unruly creatures to keep on the straight and narrow, huh? Of course, what would all those beings say if they were to find out who you keep company with?"

Instead of yelling at Death, Lam sighed and continued to look out of the window. "It's far more complicated than you'd ever be able to understand, Death. I'm not here to talk about my situation."

"I can just guess why you finally decided to show up." Death huffed as he sat up and climbed off the bed to join Lam by the window. "Are you here to punish me or to take Pierre away?"

"Why would I take Pierre away? As astonishing as it might seem, you're good for him. When was his last hit?"

Death thought about it. "The day before yesterday. He seemed tired this morning, so I told him to take a nap. I did offer him the last baggie last night, but he turned me down. Said he could deal with the symptoms. We'll see if he can deal with the boredom of being out here without wanting to shoot up."

Lam laughed, and Death was struck by how beautiful the messenger angel was. Yet there seemed to be an air of sadness around him that hadn't been there before.

Before he could stop himself, he reached out and laid his hand on Lam's shoulder.

"You do know if you need any help any time, I'll be there for you. I've been a cold bastard most of the time we've known each other, and you have no reason to believe me, but I'm telling the truth. I will help you the best I can if you ever need me."

Lam covered his hand with his own and flashed him a smile. "Thank you. I hope we figure out what the hell we're doing before I end up needing your help."

Death squeezed Lam's shoulder before stepping away. "If you're not here to bust my ass about Pierre, why are you here?"

Lam went to sit in one of the chairs in front of the fireplace. The angel crossed his legs and folded his hands in his lap. All Lam needed was a pair of glasses perched on the end of his nose and he'd look like the therapist Pierre always harped about. Death had the urge to lie down on the couch and pour out his messed-up soul to Lam.

"I'm here simply to look in on you both and make sure things are progressing. You seemed very determined to save him, and I know Pierre was looking for a reason to be saved. You just have to make sure he doesn't become as dependent on you as he did on the drugs. The withdrawal symptoms, once you leave, could end up being worse than those from the heroin."

"I know," Death admitted, tugging on the hem of his shirt like a little kid. "I'm trying to keep him from getting attached, but what happens when I become more attached to him than I should be? I try to remain closed off to him, but he reminds me of someone I loved, and it's messing with my mind."

Lam tilted his head, a puzzled frown marring his perfect forehead. "I've never seen you like this, Death.

Usually none of the souls you're sent to take affect you like this. What is it about Pierre that's causing you to have doubts about your job?"

Death shook his head. "Oh, I don't have doubts about my job. If you need me to go somewhere, I'll go, but what if I don't want to let him go? What if I want him to sleep in my bed with me?"

He paced the length of his room, not enjoying the fact he was spilling his guts to Lam, but he didn't have anyone else to talk to, and maybe talking would help clear up some of the confusion in his head.

"Well, that does make things a little sticky."

Death snorted, and Lam rolled his eyes.

"Grow up and pay attention. Death, you have to make sure you like Pierre for being Pierre, not this person you used to love. Using Pierre, even with the best of intentions, will only end up hurting him in the end."

"I know that, and I also know I can't keep him. He'll have to return to his world soon enough, but I want him to stay here. I've always been a solitary man, guarding my privacy with jealous regard. Yet I've opened my world to him. Hell, I've brought Pierre here, when I've never brought any man except for Oliver here to spend time with me." Death shoved his hands through his hair, tugging on the ends in frustration.

Lam hummed, and Death hated the sound. Silence built between them until Death wanted to scream at the angel, yet he controlled himself. Lam didn't deserve to bear the brunt of Death's confused anger.

Finally, Lam sighed and stood. The angel approached him and took his hands in his. "I wish I could give you the right answer, or even any kind of answer, but I can't. There are powers at work here I don't understand and don't wish to know."

Death reared back, staring at Lam. "What are you talking about?"

"I can't tell you."

"Can't or won't?" Death glared.

Lam shrugged. "Can't. I told you, there are other things in play here, and I'm not privy to them. Issues and stuff I wouldn't be told about anyway. It isn't my realm of work. Just tell me you won't play with him. If you take Pierre to your bed, Death, make sure you're doing it because you want him, not whoever has been stuck in your heart. Pierre deserves to be wanted for himself."

"Yes, he does." Death jerked his hands out of Lam's and nodded toward the door. "You should leave. I have work to do before this afternoon. Excuse me if I don't escort you out."

He turned his back on the angel and stalked over to the door leading to his personal study. All he knew was his head hurt from thinking about this entire situation, and he was tired of it. Death would bury himself in simple business matters and forget his problems for a while.

Maybe if he did that, he could actually enjoy the afternoon spent in Pierre's company. As he booted up his computer, he made a quick decision. By the end of the day, he would come to a conclusion. Whether it was to leave Pierre untouched and send him home, or whether he would welcome the young mortal into his bed. After he decided either way, it would be over, and he wouldn't question himself any longer.

* * * *

They pulled the horses to a stop at the top of a gentle hill, and Death studied Pierre as the mortal gazed over the view. Pink colored Pierre's cheeks, giving him a healthy glow — something Death was pretty sure Pierre hadn't had in a long time. Pierre's auburn curls tumbled around his head in an attractive windswept appearance. It was a very good look for the young man.

"All of this is yours?" Pierre nodded toward the land in the distance.

"All of it up to the road. It's about a hundred acres, which isn't nearly as much as I had when I was mortal, but still its more than most people have." Death settled back in the saddle, resting his hands on the pommel while letting the reins hang loose. His horse stretched its neck. "I lease some land to a local farmer since I don't need it. Mostly, I spend my time riding while I'm out here."

"I can see why. This is beautiful," Pierre murmured.

"Come on. There's a spot I want to show you."

Death gathered his reins and turned his mount to the left before nudging the gelding into a trot. He heard the hoof beats of Pierre's horse, so he wasn't worried about Pierre following him. They dropped down into a walk as they entered a small stand of trees surrounding a pond.

He dismounted and draped the reins over a low bush. As Pierre did the same, Death removed the saddlebags. They strolled to the edge of the pond and sat on the grass. Pierre trailed his fingers in the water, giving Death a good view of the track and red scratch marks marring Pierre's arm.

"How's the need today?"

Pierre looked to see what Death stared at and wrinkled his nose. "Worse than yesterday. Feels like I have bugs crawling under my skin."

"I'm sorry, but you've managed to go this long without another hit, why not see if you can go longer?"

"I'm taking it an hour at a time. I'm not sure when the need will settle to a dull roar in the back of my mind, but I'm willing to try and see." Pierre gestured to the bags. "What did you bring?"

Death unpacked some cheese, pear and apple slices, and a small bottle of wine. "I thought we could use an afternoon snack."

"Great. I'm starving." Pierre chuckled. "Christ, I can remember when I'd go days without eating. Heroin was the only thing I needed to stay alive."

Nodding, Death handed Pierre a small plate of cheese and fruit. "Yeah, you can stand to gain another forty pounds or so, but don't worry. With the magician I have as cook in this house, you won't have any problem gaining the weight. Heck, I have to be careful how much I eat when I'm here."

Their joined laughter filled the spring air, and Death forced away memories of making snow angels with Oliver the one time he'd brought the man out to the country. He poured them a glass of wine each, took a sip and set the glass down before leaning back on his hands and stretching his legs out in front of him.

"Tell me about yourself, Pierre. All I know is this moment of time in your life. Tell me what led up to it."

He wasn't sure if Pierre would be open to talking about himself, but Death figured it would be the best way to lance some of the emotional wounds Pierre carried around. Pierre fiddled with the plate, pushing the food around it.

"You could probably find all this stuff out on the net," Pierre pointed out.

"I could find out the surface things, and while that stuff is important, I want to know all the underlying things going on in your world. When did you start using, and what made you decide drugs were better than just living through the pain?" Death took a bite of cheese, trying to act like it wasn't important if Pierre told him anything or not.

Silence fell over them, and Death didn't feel the need to break it. He'd spent days in silence, because he didn't have friends to chat with or someone to talk to all the time. Before the internet or even telephones, he'd go weeks without talking to anyone. Silence didn't bother him.

Finally Pierre broke it with a sigh. "You probably know Jameson is my stepfather."

"Yes." No elaboration. Keeping it simple wouldn't give Pierre a reason to stop talking.

"Well, my father left my mom when I was six. One day he just didn't come home from work, and Mom got a call from him, telling her he wanted a divorce. As long as she didn't fight him, he'd give her a very generous alimony check every month. Lionel Fortescue was crazy rich, but he didn't like being tied down with a wife and kid. He'd got married because his father wanted him settled."

Pierre picked up a stick and threw it into the pond. They watched the little waves ripple out from where the stick landed until they lost steam and faded.

"He divorced your mother but never got around to changing his will? I saw his entire fortune went to you when he died," Death admitted.

The laugh escaping from Pierre's throat was cynical and harsh. "Grandpa Fortescue was a wily bastard. Somehow he figured out Lionel married Mom to make him happy, and that wasn't what Grandpa had wanted. Ended up he wrote Lionel out of his will, except for a rather nice trust fund, and left the bulk of his empire to his only grandson."

"So when Robertson married your mother, he was also marrying the Fortescue money," Death muttered.

Pierre shook his head. "No. Again, remember Grandpa was cunning. Mom was one of three trustees named in Grandpa's will. They were in charge of my fortune until I turned twenty-five, which was earlier this year. Anyway, Jameson couldn't get his hands on any of my money. It didn't matter because Jameson is rich in his own right. He didn't need my money. No, theirs was a love match."

"Well, that's a good thing at least. Your mom has someone who loves her. I don't remember much about my parents. Nannies, governesses and tutors raised me until I reached majority. After that, I traveled the world until it was time to come home to launch my sister into society."

"Why didn't your mother do that?" Pierre frowned. "From what I remember of English history, the mother was more responsible for that sort of thing. I assume it was the same way for French society."

"My parents were world travelers. Father had lots of family money, so he took Mother on his travels, and they were never home. I ran our estates since I was eighteen, even though I tried to travel as much as I could because I knew I'd be tied down as well, once Emilia turned eighteen."

He smiled when he thought about his sister.

Chapter Eight

Pierre spied the smile crossing Death's face, and a strange rush of loneliness swept through him. "You're lucky. You had a sibling to help with the loneliness. It was just my mom and me. It wasn't like we had a rough life or anything like that. The estate gave her money, so she didn't have to work, though since I was already in school, she found a part-time job to keep from getting bored. It was how she met Jameson."

Death hummed softly but didn't speak. Pierre didn't know if the Horseman was giving him a chance to continue, or if Death was lost in his own memories.

"I was ten when Jameson swept Mom off her feet and became her Prince Charming." He winced at the bitterness in his tone. No wonder people thought he was an ungrateful wretch.

"And you were no longer two. There was a third person there to take even more of your mother's attention away." Death put into words what the ten-year-old version of Pierre had thought when his mom had married again.

"Yeah. I guess I shouldn't have been so upset because Jameson made her happy. He still does, but Mom always used to say it was us against the world, and I was her little man. All of a sudden there was another man to fight her battles for her." He held up his hand to stop Death from saying anything. "I know I wasn't old enough to actually do anything to help her, but I thought I was. I thought I was all she needed to make her happy."

He sipped his wine, staring at the calm surface of the pond. The water was so clear; he could see small fish swimming around near the bottom. The quietness of the place seeped into him, and he realized it was the first time in a long time he'd had a picnic by a pond. In fact, it had been years since he'd spent any time not doing anything except drinking wine in the country without a crowd of hangers-on, or tabloid cameramen trying to take his picture.

Something in his soul drank up the silence and eased the low-level itching under his skin. Pierre couldn't remember ever feeling this easy in his own body. Was it because of the wine and the fresh country air with no sense of needing to be somewhere else? Was it because of Death lying next to him, quiet and non-judgmental, content to sit with him without needing anything else from him?

"They left me behind with the servants when they went on their honeymoon. There weren't any family members who could be bothered to take a kid for two weeks. Again, a parent abandoned me. Silly really, because Mom still loved me, but her new husband was more important than I was."

"Not a good track record, huh?" Death stroked his fingers over Pierre's hand.

"No." Pierre shrugged and turned his hand over to trap Death's fingers in his.

Death didn't try to free his hand. He tightened his grip, and Pierre slid closer to Death. Another tug, and he lay next to Death, resting his head on the Horseman's chest. He closed his eyes, absorbing Death's warmth and letting the sound of his breathing calm him.

"I shouldn't have been surprised, you know. Lionel found it really easy to forget about me. I never heard or saw him once the divorce was final. It was like I no longer existed in the world." Pierre exhaled slowly.

"Then your mother seemed to be doing the exact same thing, and you couldn't figure out why you were so easy to forget. You know, if I'd had time to think when I was younger, I might have felt the same way you did. But I had to take care of my sister and the estate, so I didn't have any time to wish things were different."

Pierre frowned. "Is that a comment on how difficult everyone has it? I shouldn't be pouting because at least I had money and didn't have to worry about food, and shit like that?"

Death laughed, and Pierre's head bounced up and down on Death's chest.

"No. I'm not thinking that at all. I was a rich kid as well, and my parents weren't around much either. But I had someone else to care about, and other things to occupy my time, so I didn't get a chance to think about how worthless I must be because no one was around to love me."

"I know you grew up in an entirely different era than I did, but did anyone else know you liked men?"

He looked up at Death and saw him lift one shoulder in a half shrug.

"Only my sister, and that's because she was around when the man I loved died. She held me while I fell apart that night. No one else knew it for sure, because I could have been put to death for it. Back in my time, it was illegal for two men to be together in a sexual way. Oh, people knew we existed, and some pleasure houses had male whores to cater to those of us with 'perverse' tastes."

Pierre pushed up on one hand and stared down at Death. "But if someone had found out and wanted to make trouble for you, they could have reported you."

"Yes, and I could have been killed. In some ways, the world has become a much more accepting place, and in other ways, it hasn't changed at all."

Their gazes met and held. Desire shot through Pierre, and he licked his lips, wanting nothing more than to lean down and kiss Death. He wasn't sure how the Horseman would react. He had never rejected any of Pierre's advances. Death just hadn't taken them to their conclusion. Maybe Death didn't want him that way, and it was easier to turn away than to say no outright.

Death reached up and slid his hand over Pierre's nape, pulling him down. Their lips met, and Pierre couldn't keep the groan back. Death shoved, and in a surge of strength Pierre found himself on his back with Death on top of him. He spread his legs, letting Death settle between them. Pierre arched, rubbing his groin against Death's, and groaned. All he could think about was having Death buried as deep as possible inside him.

"God, you smell so good," Death murmured as he nuzzled Pierre's chin.

Pierre blinked, not sure what Death was talking about. He didn't smell any different than he usually did. When Death shoved Pierre's collar out of the way and bit down on the muscle connecting his shoulder to his neck, Pierre realized he didn't care. If Death thought he smelled good, then great. All he wanted was them naked soon.

"Naked. Please," he begged, tugging on Death's shirt.

After rocking back on his heels, Death unbuttoned the top couple of buttons and pulled his shirt over his head. Pierre did the same, and their shirts were thrown aside. Pierre bit his lip, praying he wouldn't come when Death lowered his lightly furred chest to Pierre's, and his chest hair tickled Pierre's sensitive nipples. Christ, it was the oddest thing how badly he wanted Death inside him. Almost like the overwhelming craving for heroin.

Death bit Pierre's chin while he trailed kisses down to the middle of Pierre's chest. Pierre ran his fingers through Death's hair, tugging it loose from the string tying it back. He buried his hands in the silken length as Death licked a wet circle around one of his nipples, drawing a low cry from him.

His eyes drifted closed, and he welcomed the pleasure and lust sweeping through him with each touch of Death's lips and tongue on his nipples. Neither side was ignored until Pierre writhed under Death, begging for something he couldn't put into words. His nipples were red and aching by the time Death decided to move on.

"We need to get these off you," Death announced while he ran the tip of his finger down the bulge in Pierre's jeans.

"Oh God, yes."

Pierre sat up and struggled with his boots for a few seconds before Death took pity on him.

"Here. Let me help you. Your hands are shaking too hard." Death paused for a moment, studying him closely. "You're not having tremors from withdrawal or anything like that?"

Pierre shook his head. "No. The symptoms this time weren't nearly as bad as they were the last two times I tried to get clean. Maybe because I didn't go cold turkey."

"Hmmm…" Death hummed, still not looking convinced.

Pierre grabbed him by the ears and kissed him hard, demanding Death take him seriously. He didn't want the Horseman to think he was fragile or broken to the point Death wouldn't fuck him.

Death chuckled when they broke apart. "All right, Pierre. I get the idea. Let's get naked and see where it all goes from there."

"Good. I'm dying here." Pierre gestured to his erection still trapped in his jeans.

"Oh, poor thing," Death murmured, patting the bulge lightly.

Pierre growled, and Death winked at him before removing Pierre's boots and tossing them to the side. Quicker than Pierre could think, he was naked, and Death wedged his shoulders between Pierre's legs. Pierre wanted to do the same with Death. He wanted the Horseman as bare and exposed as he was, but he couldn't get his hands and mind to work together. Then all thought escaped as Death wrapped his lips around Pierre's cock and sucked him down.

"Holy shit!" Pierre shouted, digging his fingers into the ground they lay on.

Death peered up at him with what was probably a smirk, but the expression was ruined by the fact he had his face buried in the hair at the base of Pierre's shaft. Death began to bob up and down, applying a crazy amount of suction. It was fast becoming the best blow job Pierre had ever gotten.

He snarled when Death released him and moved away. "What the fuck?"

Death grabbed the saddlebags and dug through them. "Here. Open the lube and put some on my fingers."

Pierre managed to catch the bottle of slick before it hit him in the face. He fumbled the lube while Death returned to his previous position and what he'd been doing. Pierre popped open the top, and Death held out his hand. He squirted lube onto Death's fingers without spilling it all over the place. He was proud of himself for being able to multitask while his dick was in someone else's mouth.

He dropped the bottle next to them, not caring what happened to it, because Death used his other hand to lift Pierre's ass off the ground. Pierre whimpered as Death trailed his wet fingers over Pierre's crease, coming to a stop at Pierre's hole.

"Yes, please. I want your fingers there, or your tongue, but mostly I want your cock there as soon as possible. Christ! I need something to fill me, Death. You're killing me here."

Death's snort caused him to focus on what he'd just said. He rolled his eyes and waved a hand at his lover.

"Just ignore me. I tend to babble when I'm having a good time." Pierre was proud of being able to form full sentences.

Death rubbed his fingers over Pierre's puckered opening, and again all ability to think disappeared. Pierre spread his legs even more, angling his hips to give Death easier access to any part of him the Horseman wanted.

Pierre became lost in the sensations of Death's mouth and fingers. One surrounding him in moist heat, and the other filling him. He didn't know how many fingers

Death had breached him with, but it wasn't quite enough. Pierre rocked between Death's mouth and fingers, babbling as his climax built along his spine. He was going to splinter into a million pieces when he came. He could only trust Death would be able to put him back together when it was over.

"Death, I'm gonna…" He tried to gasp out a warning.

A slight shake of his head was all Death did to tell him he didn't care. His climax tore through him, and Pierre cried out, filling the country air with his joy. He thrust and rocked, flooding Death's mouth with his cum. Death drank it down without hesitation. Pierre closed his eyes, allowing the sensation ripple over him. God, it was better than heroin.

After it felt like the last drop had been sucked out of him, he flopped to the ground, panting. Death stood, stripped off his own pants, and dug around the saddlebags again. Pierre couldn't form a coherent thought about what the Horseman searched for. The crinkle of foil brought his gaze from the sky to where Death knelt between his thighs again.

"Are you ready?" Death reached for the lube, squirted some on his palm and coated his rubber-covered cock.

Pierre grunted and gained control of his body enough to catch his knees. He pulled them up and back, offering his ass up to Death without doubt or worry. Death wasn't going to hurt him, and as weird as it sounded, he believed Death wasn't just using him.

"Yes."

Death positioned his cock at Pierre's hole and slowly pressed in. Pierre let his head drop back onto the grass as he tried to relax. Death had done a good job stretching him, but Death's cock was still bigger than the Horseman's fingers. He bit his lip and breathed deep until Death was buried as far inside him as he could go. Death braced his hands on either side of Pierre's head and leaned down to press a kiss to Pierre's mouth.

Their breath mingled, and Pierre gripped the back of Death's head. Pierre stroked his tongue in and out of Death's mouth, mimicking what Death was doing to him with his cock. Death hit Pierre's gland, and Pierre broke their kiss, crying out as electricity shot through him.

"You're so tight," Death murmured. "You fit like a glove around me."

They undulated together, thrusting and shoving. Pierre massaged Death's cock with his inner muscles, driving the Horseman closer and closer to the edge. Death's breathing sped up, and his smooth rhythm became jerky. Pierre's cock seemed to think about getting hard again, but even with the steady nailing his gland was getting, his own climax had taken a lot out of him. He didn't mind though, as long as Death came.

Finally, Death groaned and flooded the condom. Pierre wrapped his arms around Death as the Horseman collapsed on top of him. He ran his fingers up and down Death's sweat-covered back. Pierre whispered love words, not even knowing what he said. He just wanted to soothe Death.

As their heartbeats calmed and their strength returned, Death slid out and took care of the condom. After grabbing his T-shirt, Pierre pushed to his feet and went to the pond's edge. He dipped the shirt in the water and washed off before handing the wet fabric to Death. The Horseman used it to clean up and tucked it away in a plastic bag with the rest of their trash.

Pierre and Death lay together after washing and dressing. Death had given Pierre his shirt to wear. After rolling the sleeves up, Pierre rested his chin on his fists, which were propped on Death's chest.

"How old were you when you became Death?"

Death met his eyes for a moment, and Pierre could practically see the wheels turning in his head. Finally, Death blinked and turned his face away.

"I was thirty-five when I died," Death said.

"How did you die?"

"Are you sure you want to know?" Death focused at Pierre, his dark gaze burning.

"Sure. It can't be that bad. I mean, unless you were dismembered or something like that." Pierre paused as a thought hit him. "You weren't beheaded with a guillotine or something?"

Death tilted his head. "Why haven't you called me crazy? Or run away screaming once you weren't high anymore?"

Pierre chuckled. "It would have been smarter, huh? As my previous actions have shown, I don't always do the wise thing."

"True."

"I figured you might be crazy, but you haven't tried to hurt me. So it might be better for me to stay with you than to wander around Paris searching for a dealer." Pierre poked Death in the stomach with his finger. "Now quit stalling and tell me about how you died."

Death inhaled, lifting Pierre as his chest expanded. Pierre kept staring at Death, not letting the Horseman off the hook.

"Fine. I was on my way home from a very late night at one of my clubs. I should have taken my carriage home, but I wanted to walk, and it wasn't that far away from where I lived. I'd had a little too much to drink, which was the story of my life at the time." Death frowned.

Pierre cleared his throat. "Were you an alcoholic?"

"In modern terms, yes, I was. I freely admit it, and if I hadn't been killed that night, I might have eventually died from too much drink."

"But you drink now," Pierre pointed out.

Death nodded. "Yes, and I don't get drunk, so I tend not to drink nearly as much. Anyway, I was accosted on the street, dragged into an alley and beaten to death."

"Did they try to rob you, and you wouldn't give them anything?" Pierre tried to think of reasons why Death's attack would have happened.

Death shook his head. "I thought it was a robbery, but turns out they were getting me back for killing a man earlier that day."

"You killed someone?"

Pierre sat up and stared down at Death. While the Horseman came across as cold and uncaring, Pierre couldn't see him killing anyone. Death sat up as well, draping his arms over his knees, and staring out over the pond.

"Yes, I did. I'd killed a couple of men. Mostly brigands or highwaymen trying to steal from me, but the man I killed that morning was a nobleman, or at least he was in title, if not actions."

Pierre frowned, not sure how he felt about that. "What did he do to you?"

"He did nothing physically to me. I took exception to what he did to my sister. St. Lucian raped her, and I demanded satisfaction. We fought a duel in one of the parks, and I shot him in the chest. He died a few hours later. His family, a more unsavory bunch of bastards I'd never met, hired some ruffians to kill me." Death shrugged before he stood, holding out his hand to Pierre. "I don't regret what I did to St. Lucian. He had to pay for what he did to Emilia. Honestly, the only thing I regret out of the whole situation is the fact I ended up as Death, instead of simply dead."

Pierre let Death help him up, but stayed silent as they gathered up their stuff and climbed astride their mounts. Death led the way back toward the house. Pierre followed behind, staring at Death's back and trying to figure out how he felt about the fact Death had killed a man. While he understood why Death would try to revenge the violation of his sister, he didn't understand why he would fight a duel. Of course, he didn't have a sibling to take care of.

"Was your sister okay?"

Death shot him a glance over his shoulder. "Okay? What, do you mean after he raped her?"

"Yeah." Pierre waved a hand, not entirely sure what he meant.

"She wouldn't let me bring a doctor to examine her, but the bruises faded. She had moments of anger and tears. Emilia let her emotions take control once in a while. Yet I forgave her most of the time because I understood she was hurt and fearful." Death looked away. "She was far more emotional and personable than me. I was the adult, so I had to be the tough one."

Pierre wrinkled his nose, wishing he had been around when Death was whoever he had been. He would have helped him out, or at least tried to be a friend to him. Yet Pierre had learned a little about himself, and he admitted he might not have been any help to Death. Pierre could barely take care of himself.

"Did you have any friends?"

They arrived at the stables, and the groom who had brought out the horses took their reins. Pierre patted his horse on the shoulder before heading into the house with Death.

"Why didn't you ride your gray horse?"

Death swung around, put his finger to his mouth, and shook his head. Johnson stepped into the library just as they walked through the French doors.

"Dinner will be served at seven sharp, sir. I'm sure you and Master Pierre would like to clean up and change before then."

"Thank you, Johnson. I appreciate it, and we'll be down at six-thirty for a drink."

Death rested his hand at the small of Pierre's back as they went upstairs. They stopped outside Pierre's suite, and Death looked at him.

"You're more than welcome to share my shower with me."

"I'd love to." Pierre pushed up on his toes and kissed Death. "Let me grab a change of clothes and I'll join you in a second."

"Certainly."

Death left as Pierre entered his room. After shutting the door, Pierre leaned against it and pressed his fingers to his lips. Somehow Death had managed not to answer his last two questions, but Pierre decided he'd just keep asking until Death answered him.

He pushed away from the door and went to the closet where he grabbed a pair of slacks and a button-down shirt. Dinner was probably a more formal event than lunch. Pierre remembered having to dress for dinners at his parents' house. He stopped by his dresser and got some underwear and socks. Maybe Death would have a tie he could borrow.

Pierre left his room and went to Death's, which was empty. He heard the water running in the bathroom and assumed Death was already in there. Pierre stripped off Death's shirt, setting it on a chair in the corner before removing his pants and folding them. As he strolled into the bathroom, he looked at his reflection in the large full-length mirror on one of the walls.

He hadn't looked at himself in the last couple of days. Mostly because he'd known how much weight he'd lost over the year and half before he'd ended up in Paris. Somehow he'd become ugly, and he knew the others only stuck with him because of the drugs and money he could get them. None of them were interested in helping him overcome his addictions since they had the same ones.

He doubted any of his so-called friends had worried when he'd disappeared. More than likely, they moved on to the next easy mark, yet he couldn't bring himself to care. They'd never done anything for him, so why should he care what had become of them?

Death slipped his arms around Pierre's waist and drew him back against his wet body. "I thought you were going to join me."

"I am. Just got a little distracted." Turning, he pressed tight to Death and kissed him.

"You distract me all the time. Come on." Death took his hand and led him into the walk-in shower.

Pierre glanced around him with his mouth open. It was the biggest shower he'd ever seen with multiple heads on all the walls, shooting cascades of water all over him. Death had the streams about waist high, though he probably readjusted them to wash his hair.

They reveled in the water, teasing and laughing as they washed. When the shower finally ran cold, they climbed out and dried off. As they dressed, Pierre thought how different his time spent with Death was. There wasn't any thought of what he needed to do for the Horseman to keep him happy or around even.

Death liked Pierre for some strange reason, and Pierre wasn't going to look a gift horse in the mouth.

Chapter Nine

Death strolled along the hallway, heading toward the library where he knew Pierre would be. The past week had been marvelous — the best days of Death's life since he became a Horseman. They'd spent the time talking, and Death had discovered Pierre was actually a very intelligent man, just dealing with a lack of focus at times. The addiction seemed to have faded. Not disappeared, because Death knew an addiction never really went away. It would be something Pierre fought all of his life.

He pushed open the library door and glanced around the edge to see Pierre sitting in one of the window seats, talking on the phone. Death stepped in, and Pierre looked up at him with a smile.

"Hey, Mom, I have to go. Don't worry. I'll call you again tomorrow, and we'll talk about when I'll be heading home." Pierre paused as his mom talked. "I'm clean, Mom. Have been for over a week now. It's tough, but I'm finding other ways to deal with the craving."

His mom must have said goodbye because he hung up while Death approached. Pierre moved his legs so

Death could join him on the seat. Death took the phone and tucked it in his pocket before taking Pierre's hand in his.

"How's your mother doing?"

Pierre smiled. "She's doing well. Still wants me to come home right away, but I told her I had to hang out on my own for a while. I have to make sure this new-found sobriety sticks."

"You do realize you haven't really been tested yet." Death studied Pierre. "I don't do drugs, and I'm not hassling you to try them. Do you think you'll be able to handle a crowd of so-called friends pressuring you into doing a line or shooting some up?"

Pierre gazed out over the beautiful gardens spread out from the side of the house. Some of the flowers were just beginning to bloom, and Death knew in another month or so the gardens would be an explosion of color.

"I know it's easy to be positive here, and swear I'll never touch another needle or snort another line, but I feel different this time. I'm stronger." Pierre looked back at him. "Maybe because you're here with me."

"Don't count on me, Pierre. I won't always be here. For some reason, these last weeks have been quiet. Normally, I'm not around much at all. I travel all over the world doing my job."

"Why don't you ride your gray horse around here?"

Pierre had asked that question when they'd first arrived at the country house, but Death had managed not to answer it. He chose to avoid it because he thought the less Pierre knew about the Horsemen, the less likely it would be he'd have his memory erased by the end of this.

What could answering this one question hurt?

It had been a while since Oliver's voice danced through his head, and Death had hoped it meant his imaginary friend was gone.

"He really isn't mine, and when I'm not using him as Death, he goes away."

"Where does he go?" Pierre frowned.

Death lifted his shoulder in a slight shrug. "I don't know. It's not like he can tell me, and Lam always says it's none of my business where the horses go. Of course, they aren't real horses. They're creatures created for the Horsemen to use when they're needed. I think they're spirits."

Pierre played with Death's fingers as he thought. What had him thinking so hard?

"I saw that blond guy you call Lam before," Pierre confessed.

"Yeah. You saw him the night I took you from the hotel room." Death tugged until Pierre crawled over into his lap. "When he showed up, I thought for sure he was there to stop me."

Pierre shook his head. "No. Before that, he and the guy you called Day were in my hotel room. I think they were even the ones who got me the tainted heroin."

"I doubt it, Pierre. I can't see Lam giving a junkie drugs, and while Day might do something like that if he wanted your soul, he didn't seem all that interested in it the last time I saw him." Death doubted Lam would have been anywhere near Pierre before Death showed up. It didn't make sense.

"You might be right. I was high both times, so maybe I just got it all mixed up in my mind." Pierre laid his hand on Death's chest, over his heart. "You know I was thinking about another of my questions you never answered. You're really good at deflecting stuff you don't want to talk about."

He could only imagine what Pierre wanted to talk about, and yes, most of it Death didn't want to discuss. Yet if he expected Pierre to talk about what was bothering him, Death had to do the same.

"What did you want to ask me?"

"Did you have any friends when you were mortal? Or were you too shut off or closed down to let anyone in?"

Death ran his hand up the outside of Pierre's thigh, fighting the instinct to distract Pierre with a kiss or something like that. He leaned his head back against the windowpane and sighed.

"No. I only had one person I considered a friend, and I treated him so poorly, I couldn't risk doing that to another person."

Pierre rested his head on Death's shoulder, snuggling in close and encircling Death's waist with his arm. "Tell me about your friend. Is he the one who died while you were somewhere else?"

"Yes."

He didn't want to talk about Oliver, not to Pierre or anyone else for that matter. For centuries he'd kept Oliver close to his heart, never allowing his memories out in the open.

"Maybe it's time you let me out and let me go, Gatian. Four hundred years seem rather a long time to hold a memory."

"I met Oliver when I was twenty-eight. I'd returned to Paris because Emilia was turning eighteen, and I needed to present her to society. Not something I was comfortable with, but she was my sister, so I was willing to support her." Death snorted. "I didn't understand the whole process of society and the Season, where young girls are paraded around by their mothers in order to snare a rich or titled husband."

"Maybe you didn't understand it because you weren't interested in any of those young girls." Pierre poked him in the stomach.

Death chuckled. "You could be right about that. I think I was far more interested in their brothers."

"Was Oliver one of those brothers?"

How did Death describe Oliver? How did one describe the first person to steal his heart and to break it as well?

"No. Oliver had been the youngest son of a country farmer. He'd come to the city to find work."

"Such a sad tale, and like so many others in those times."

He wanted to tell Oliver to shut up, but since he didn't think it was really his old lover's voice, he didn't want to end up talking to himself.

"You met him at his job?"

"You could say that. Like many innocent girls and boys coming in from the country, the wrong person befriended Oliver. He was drugged and found himself in a pleasure house. I bought his services for a night after he'd been working there for five years."

Pierre straightened up and stared at him. "You paid for a prostitute?"

Death didn't look away. Modern mores had made him ashamed of paying for sex, but back when he was mortal, he'd done it all the time. He'd made sure he'd used reputable pleasure houses, and he'd never taken an unwilling lover. Of course, there were distinct possibilities a lot of the whores he'd used were unwilling, but they never showed it to him.

"Yes, I did. You have to understand, Pierre, it was a different time than you live in now. Men like us weren't supposed to be welcomed in polite society. Oh, others knew we existed, and we were allowed to be part of society because of our titles or our fortunes. Yet our perversions couldn't be talked about or seen. It was easier to pay for sex than to risk approaching someone who could get me killed."

Pierre blinked as he nodded. "I guess you're right about that. Was that why you asked if I had sex for money? And why you told me you wouldn't judge me if I had?"

"Yes. I don't think there's anything wrong with prostitution in general, and because it would make me a hypercritic in specifics. I'll admit I'm not happy you sold yourself for drugs. Like I said, you sold yourself too cheaply." Death grimaced. "I have no room to say anything against you since I've bought men for sex."

Pierre looked at Death with a piercing glance. "Something tells me, though, you only paid because you didn't want to develop any feelings for the man you slept with. If you spent the night in another lord's bed, it could be easy to get used to being with him, and you didn't want to be tied down."

"I only wanted to get Emilia married, then I planned on taking off for other countries." Death closed his eyes again, and an image of Oliver, sex-tossed and drowsy, skated across his mind. "But then I met Oliver, and all bets were off. Emilia didn't take well her first season, so we stayed in Paris and kept trying to find her the right husband. She loved being in the city. I loved being able to spend my nights in Oliver's bed, listening to him beg me to fuck him."

"And you did it so well. You were by far my favorite patron."

Death bit his lip to keep from saying anything. When he was mortal and Oliver was alive, he'd hated thinking about Oliver lying underneath another man, getting fucked by anyone other than him.

"Oliver was a willing whore then?"

Death wanted to yell at Pierre that Oliver wasn't a whore, but he couldn't. Oliver was a whore, and nothing Death said could convince Oliver to leave the pleasure house.

"Yes, he was for me anyway. I don't know what he was like for his other customers. Well, any of the others except for the man who killed him."

"He was killed by a guy who paid to fuck him?" Pierre shook his head. "That's screwed up, man."

"I know, and I don't know what happened. I tried to find out the truth, but the madam of the pleasure house wouldn't talk to me about Oliver. The man who killed him was a nobleman, and she couldn't risk losing his patronage or that of his friends. Oliver didn't matter to her except as loss of income, and she could collect another innocent farm boy from the coach houses."

Pierre growled low in his throat. "That seems so unfair. I don't understand why the rich are always protected like that."

"It's always that way. Unfortunately, in France, the power of the rich caused their downfall in my time. The French Revolution was so bloody, and unbelievably sad. So many died who didn't have to, but once blood lust is fired, there is rarely any way to stop it except to let it burn out."

Death thought about the blood spilt during the Revolution. All the people imprisoned and hauled to the guillotine for no other reason than they had a title, and maybe more money than most. Not all of the noble families were bad or corrupt, but once the people were roused, it didn't matter.

"Did you do anything to Oliver's killer? I'm assuming you found out who did it."

Pierre's question brought Death back to the conversation at hand. He smiled, and from the way Pierre's eyes widened at the sight, Death knew it was rather an evil one.

"Yes. I found out who killed Oliver, though no one would tell me why. I hunted the nobleman down and thrashed him. I probably would have killed him, but I came to my senses."

"You should have killed him. It wasn't right he got away with killing Oliver." Pierre sounded indignant.

"Don't worry, you blood-thirsty Hun. I punished him in a way that caused him far more lingering pain than simply killing him. Causing his death would have been easy and relatively painless for him. No, I wanted him to suffer as long as possible, since I wouldn't be getting over Oliver's death any time soon."

Pierre rested his hand against Death's cheek with a gentle touch. "I don't think you've ever gotten over it."

Death dropped his gaze, but he didn't protest because Pierre was right. He hadn't recovered from Oliver's death.

"What did you do after you beat the shit out of the asshole?"

"I did my level best to get him shunned by society, and it worked. People believed what I told them and turned from him. He became a pariah, and when I took all his money, he ceased to exist in the eyes of society. I ruined him." Death tried to tamp down the surge of pride in his soul at the thought of what he'd done to the man.

"Remind me not to piss you off," Pierre teased.

"To be honest, no one could point to me as the origin of the rumors about him being discovered in a delicate situation with a certain male personage at a certain pleasure house. I didn't lie about him, just placed a bug in a certain matron's ear and let the viciousness of mortals take over." Death scratched his chin. "He was the one who ran up debts and gambled with money he didn't have. I merely bought up his markers and called them. I don't think he ever knew why I hated him."

Pierre swung around until he straddled Death's lap, and Death grasped Pierre's butt in his hands. He stared into those gold-green eyes and breathed in the oddly familiar scent he'd always attributed to Oliver. There were so many things about Pierre that reminded Death of his dead lover, yet so many things were different.

"Doesn't it bother you that you ruined this man's life?" Pierre tilted his head like Death's answer was the most important thing he'd hear all day.

Death shook his head. "Should it? Listen, I killed the man who raped my sister. I couldn't kill the man who caused Oliver's death, but I could ruin him, so he lost everything he cared about in his life. It's what I do to protect those I love, even though it's usually after the fact. If someone hurts someone I care about, I will do everything in my power to destroy the person."

Silence filled the air after Death's vow. Pierre slowly started unbuttoning Death's shirt, but Death could tell there was something else besides sex on Pierre's mind. He didn't push because he'd learned Pierre would talk about it in his own time.

He smoothed his palms over Pierre's tight ass up and around to the button at Pierre's waistband. Pierre sucked in his stomach, giving Death room to get his fingers into Pierre's jeans and get them undone. Death's shirt parted, and he grunted as Pierre leaned forward to brush a kiss over one of his nipples.

Pinching Pierre's side, he grinned as his lover jerked, and glared at him.

"Get these off." He tugged on the jeans. "We haven't fucked in several hours, and I find I'm more interested in your ass at the moment than any more emotional sharing."

"Yes, sir."

Pierre jumped to his feet and shimmied out of his jeans. Death's mouth watered at the sight before him. Pierre was beautifully made, and with the weight he'd added over the last couple of weeks, he was perfect. Still lean, but muscular, Pierre didn't look sick anymore. Pierre tore off his T-shirt and flung it across the room like a stripper. Death reached out and flicked Pierre's nipple, drawing a low cry from him.

"No underwear? You are a bit of a hedonist, aren't you?"

Death removed his shirt and pants before crooking a finger at Pierre, motioning for him to come closer as Death sat back on the window seat. Pierre winked at him and dropped to his knees. He pushed Death's thighs apart so he could settle between them. Death ran his fingers through Pierre's curls, happy to see the locks had regained their luster.

Pierre seemed to have kicked his addiction quite easily, but Death wasn't fooled. It wasn't hard to ignore the urge when someone distracted you. The difficult test would be when Pierre left and re-joined the real world. Pierre would have to deal with his old circle of friends who wanted him addicted and easy to manipulate. Those were the moments where Pierre would have to stand strong.

All thoughts disappeared from Death's head when Pierre wrapped his lips around the head of Death's cock and sucked a little before taking Death all the way down. Death let his head fall back against the glass and closed his eyes. For a moment, he imagined it was Oliver kneeling between him, pleasuring him with his mouth.

"But it's not me, and you do Pierre a disservice by thinking of someone else while you're with him."

"Fuck," he muttered.

Pierre eased away and looked up at him. "What's wrong?"

"Nothing." Death ignored the voice in his head and tapped Pierre on the shoulder. "Why don't you grab the lube out of my pants? You can give me a blow job later on."

"In a hurry?"

"Just needing you right now," he admitted, and it was the truth. He was discovering Pierre was quickly becoming his drug of choice.

"Well, you're in luck. When I woke up this morning, you weren't around to help with my morning wood, so I played a little and decided to be ready in case you came looking for me later."

Death frowned, but his confusion cleared up when Pierre crawled over to Death's pants and started digging around Death's pockets with his ass up in the air. The position exposed Pierre's hole, stretched and plugged. Death slid off the window seat to his knees behind Pierre and tapped on the plug.

"Oh." Pierre shivered and handed the small tube of slick back to Death. "Please, take me soon. I don't need to be stretched anymore. Just slick yourself up and fuck me."

"What about a condom?" Death knew there had been one in the same pocket as the lube.

Pierre looked over his shoulder at him and asked, "Can you get sick?"

"Never have since I became a Horseman," Death said and shuddered at the thought of fucking Pierre bare.

Death had only used condoms once HIV and AIDS had become such an epidemic, because his mortal lovers might have thought it odd if he didn't. After having gone centuries without using one, surrounding his cock with rubber annoyed him.

"Are you sure?"

As excited as he was about the prospect of doing Pierre bare, he wouldn't force the issue if Pierre weren't absolutely positive about the whole thing.

"I'm the one who suggested it, dude. I haven't been bareback ever, and I thought this might be a good time to try it since we know you won't be giving me anything. I'm negative. I get tested all the time because of the needles and drugs."

He couldn't argue with that logic, so he squirted lube into his hand and coated his cock with it. Pierre faced forward again, resting his forehead on his hands. It was the most seductive sight Death had seen in a long time. He wrapped his fingers around the base of the plug and twisted it a little.

Pierre trembled, and a soft moan came from him. Death grinned as he made the decision to tease Pierre a little before he fucked him. He grasped the base, pulling it out until just the tip was inside Pierre, and slammed it back in, driving a cry from Pierre.

"Stop teasing, you bastard," Pierre demanded. "Fuck me already. Do you know how hard I've been all morning, waiting for you to come look for me?"

"I can't believe you talked to your mother with this in your ass," Death commented as he yanked it out.

"Holy shit!" Pierre shouted, lifting his head up and giving Death a narrow-eyed stare.

Death gripped his cock in one hand while resting the other on the curve of Pierre's ass. With one fluid thrust, he breached Pierre's lubed opening and sank in until his pubic hair scraped Pierre's skin. He paused, waiting for a sign Pierre was ready for him to move. Pierre returned his forehead to his hands and squeezed Death's shaft with his inner muscles.

Death started moving in a smooth rhythm, in and out. He tried to nail Pierre's gland with each stroke, forcing whimpers and soft cries from Pierre as he fucked him. They rocked together with Pierre pushing back every time Death thrust forward. Death ran his hand over Pierre's sweat-covered back while enjoying the sight of Pierre's body moving in front of him. He loved the heat and feel of Pierre surrounding him without the extra barrier of the latex.

"Oh my God," Pierre groaned and moved faster. "Touch me. Please."

Death reached around and encircled Pierre's erection with a tight grip.

"Yes. That's it."

Their movements slowly fractured, and Death could feel the tension building in his body. He could see Pierre's climax rippling under his skin when it exploded through his muscles. Pierre dropped his head down and grunted, spilling hot cum all over Death's hand and the floor beneath them.

Death pumped out all he could from Pierre before letting go and grabbing a hold of Pierre's hips. He reamed Pierre's ass, hard and fast, needing just a few more strokes to set his own climax off. Death buried his cock as deep as he could and froze while pleasure shot through him until stars sparkled before his eyes. His cum flooded Pierre's passage.

"Christ, that's amazing," Pierre whispered.

Death's strength gave out, and he collapsed on to Pierre, taking them both to the floor. Their whimpers mingled together when Death's soft cock slid from Pierre's ass. Pierre wiggled around until he settled into Death's embrace, and they lay there, dozing as control over their muscles returned. Death drifted along, listening to Pierre's steady breathing.

"I missed this," he said.

"Missed what?" Pierre ran his fingers along Death's abs, tracing the dips and curves of the muscles.

"Holding someone, and not just after sex. I would spend all night with Oliver, and we didn't always have sex, or at least we didn't have sex all the time. Sometimes, after we'd fucked, we would lie in each other's arms and talk."

"Ummm…don't take this the wrong way, but what does a whore have to talk about? Did he get to leave the brothel during the day or something?"

Pierre's assumption about whores didn't bother Death. He'd thought the same thing until he'd met Oliver. While Oliver's situation hadn't been perfect, Oliver had done his best to be more than just an ignorant whore.

"I'd bring him books, and between clients, he'd read. Then when I came to be with him, we would talk about what he'd read. Those times were some of the ones I came to treasure, even more than when I fucked him. I liked learning how he thought, and what he'd enjoy doing if he wasn't stuck in the pleasure house all day."

"You really did care for him, didn't you?"

Death snorted. "I ruined a man because he killed Oliver. If I hadn't loved Oliver, I would never have done any of it. I'm very protective of those who are dear to me."

Pierre hummed softly, and Death realized they were getting closer to what Pierre had been thinking before they'd made love.

"Do you care about me like that?"

Chapter Ten

Cringing, Pierre started to push away from Death. He'd wondered what Death felt about him, but he hadn't meant to ask the Horseman. Pierre wasn't naïve enough to believe Death would keep him around. The Horseman had a job to do, and Pierre was sure he'd only get in the way.

Before Death could stop him, he scrambled into his clothes and headed toward the door. "I'm going to take a shower. We should probably be dressing for dinner anyway."

"Pierre, wait," Death called, but Pierre was out of the door and down the hall.

He rushed upstairs and into his suite, locking the door behind him. Would a lock keep the Horseman from coming in if he wanted? Death didn't strike Pierre as the type of person who would force his way into some place he wasn't wanted.

Pierre stripped again, leaving his clothes scattered around the floor as he went into his bathroom and started the shower. He braced his hands on the counter, staring at his reflection in the mirror.

"Shit, Pierre. What the fuck were you thinking? Don't ask the guy fucking you if he cares about you. You know what happens when you do that. They leave or laugh, and you feel like a complete idiot for making a bigger deal of fucking than they do."

Lars had done that to him. Pierre should have known the bastard was just using him when he'd told Lars he loved him, and Lars chucked him under the chin like a little kid and called him cute.

Pierre wanted to hit his head against the wall, or shoot up with some heroin to dull his humiliation. Yet he wouldn't do either. Both ways were damaging, and he had to learn how to deal with things without hiding. He snorted as he stepped under the hot water. What was he doing now, if not hiding?

He washed up, trying not to think of how intimate it had felt to have Death take him without a condom. Hell, he'd never trusted any of the men he'd slept with to do that. Not even when he'd been higher than a kite. There was a check in the right column for him.

After turning off the water, he stepped out and dried off before heading back into his bedroom. Death stood next to his bed, dressed in a black Armani suit and wearing a very unhappy expression.

"Sorry." Pierre ducked his head and fought the urge to scuff his feet on the carpet. The fact he was buck-naked didn't help either.

"Nothing really to be sorry for. I'm upset you didn't stick around to hear my answer, but I'm not mad at you. I'm angry at Lam, and the timing of my newest mission. I wish I could stay and talk to you, because we need to talk." As he walked forward, Death took a hold of Pierre's hands and brought them up to his lips. "Please, be here when I get back, and we'll talk about everything."

Before Pierre could promise or not, a horse neighed from outside. He turned to see Death's gray stallion standing on the balcony, impatiently pawing at the stone. Pierre understood Death's explanation of the horse not being real, or maybe being a spirit. Its eyes were blood red, and it was far bigger than most horses Pierre had seen. Even if he assumed it was a real horse, something in the way it held itself told Pierre the stallion wasn't to be messed with.

"Damn it," Death swore loudly. "I thought we'd be left alone until we got you better, but I guess I was wishing on something that would never be."

Pierre kissed Death before pushing him out of the French doors. "You need to leave. I don't want your horse coming after me because I'm keeping you from something."

"Remember we have to talk when I get back, Pierre. I promise you'll like what I have to say."

Death swung astride the horse and kicked it with his heels. Neighing, the horse whirled and leaped off the balcony. In a flash of blinding light, they disappeared. Pierre stood there for a moment, staring at where Death had been. When he shivered, he remembered it was still a little chilly in the evenings, and Pierre shut the doors. He dressed and made his way downstairs to the dining room.

Johnson stood next to the table where one plate rested at the end. "Dinner is ready, sir."

Pierre sighed. "Could I just have a tray brought up to my room? I don't really feel like sitting down here by myself. Unless you'd like to join me?"

He could tell he'd surprised the man.

"No, sir. I've eaten already. I'll have one of the footmen bring a tray up for you."

"Thank you."

Pierre wandered back upstairs and went to the sitting room attached to his bedroom. He curled up in the corner of the couch, staring out of the window. He really wanted to hear what Death had to say, but he wasn't sure it was the right thing to do. Pierre should pack and go home where his parents were waiting for him.

At some point he needed to resume his life. Well, not the life he'd been leading when Death had found him. Maybe he could go to Jameson and ask for help. Jameson could help him learn how to run his grandfather's empire. It would give Pierre something to do instead of spending money on drugs and parties. Of course, he'd have to convince Jameson he meant it.

Knocking on the door brought him back to the room instead of his thoughts.

"Come in," he called.

Johnson opened the door, gesturing for a footman behind him to enter. The footman set the large tray on the table and left. Johnson placed a bottle of wine along with a glass next to it.

"Do you need anything else, Master Pierre?"

"Not tonight, Johnson. Will you have a car ready to take me back to Paris at eleven tomorrow morning? It's time I started living my life like normal people do instead of hiding away in this fairy tale castle. Also, I'll need a suitcase brought to my room."

Johnson paused at the door. "Master Almasia would prefer you stay here until he returns, Master Pierre."

"I know, but he isn't in charge of me, Johnson. I must take control of my own life. I've let too many things rule me, like the heroin or other people. I need to know I can do this on my own."

"I understand, sir, and I'll make sure the car is available. The suitcase will arrive shortly." Johnson bowed and left.

Pierre ate the delicious meal and poured a drink. He sipped the wine as he waited for a footman to bring him a suitcase. After it was brought and the tray had been taken away, Pierre finished the bottle while packing his clothes. He hated leaving while Death was gone, but he knew it was the only way. He cared about the Horseman so deeply already. If Death asked Pierre, he would stay there for as long as Death wanted.

Being a kept man wasn't what Pierre wanted to be. His actions up to this point hadn't shown it, but he wanted to make something of his life. He wanted to create or help build the world, instead of destroy it. Pierre hadn't much thought about things before, but listening to Death talk about how Oliver wanted to learn made Pierre feel like he'd wasted time partying when he could have been discovering things about his world. Being a whore who would probably never leave the pleasure house he worked in hadn't stopped Oliver from learning.

Pierre had a better life than Oliver, yet he'd wasted most of his early life having fun. He might have screwed things up at first, but he still had a lot of time to fix his problems and do something with what was left.

He set out clothes to wear the next day and climbed into bed. Curling around a pillow, he wished Death was there to hold him one last time. Something told Pierre that once he left Almasia Estate, he would never see Death again, or even be able to find him if he tried.

It was fate, or destiny, or a higher power that had brought them together. A special moment in time, and Pierre knew there wouldn't be another time like that.

Death wasn't supposed to save the souls he collected. He was supposed to take them to the gate. Pierre doubted Death had disregarded that order before, and he definitely didn't think Death would do it again.

What made Pierre different than all the other souls Death had collected over the centuries? Death had commented on his eyes, and he remembered the odd comments Death had made about how he smelled. Could Pierre remind Death of someone? Was it possible Pierre might even remind Death of his dead lover?

As thoughts and questions whirled around his brain, Pierre drifted asleep.

* * * *

Pierre rolled over and opened his eyes. Instead of seeing the ceiling he'd gotten used to over the last weeks, he saw a bright blue sky. He blinked, but the sky didn't change. He sat up and realized he wasn't in bed either. Somehow he was sitting in the middle of Death's gardens.

"Obviously this is a dream," he said.

"How did you guess?"

He twisted around and spotted a young, dark-haired man sitting a few feet away from him.

"Who are you?"

The young man studied him for a moment with startling, familiar green-gold eyes. "I think you might have a guess as to my identity."

"You're Oliver, and since you're dead, I definitely know I'm dreaming. Why would I dream about you, though?" Pierre pushed to his feet and strolled over to where Oliver sat on the bench next to a beautiful bed of red roses.

"Not sure why you would either." Oliver motioned to the bench. "I have to admit I've never had this happen to me before. I've never appeared in anyone's dreams, although I have been talking to Gatian since he met you."

Pierre joined Oliver and leaned forward, bracing his elbows on his knees. "I bet he doesn't enjoy that. What do you say to him? Is Gatian his real name?"

"Yes, it is. I don't know him as Death. I think I'm supposed to convince him he isn't responsible for my death." Oliver plucked one of the roses and removed the thorns. "These are my favorite flowers."

"Must be why Death has them all over his gardens," Pierre murmured. After a moment of quiet, he asked, "How's it working?"

"What? Convincing him?"

Pierre nodded.

Oliver shook his head. "It's not going well, though I don't think I've approached the subject the right way. I have to admit I was surprised at how badly he reacted when I died. I knew he cared for me, but I didn't think he loved me like that."

"We tend not to ever know how people really feel about us until it's too late." Pierre grunted. "Unfortunately, how they feel isn't the way we want them to feel. I found out the truth when my lover married a woman and screwed me over. At least Gatian did love you."

"Yes, he did, but I think he's falling in love with you."

"Does that bother you?" Pierre looked over at Oliver, still stunned by how beautiful the young man was.

Oliver frowned. "Why would it bother me? I'm dead."

"Good point, but he was your lover, and he hasn't forgotten you in all these centuries. I can't say the same for me. I tend to be very forgettable." Pierre pursed his lips.

Oliver punched him in the arm. "Stop feeling sorry for yourself. You're alive, and be glad for that—you came very close to dying. You still have a chance to live the life you want, instead of the life you thought you deserved."

"Ow!" Pierre rubbed the spot where Oliver had hit him. "I'm sorry. I didn't think about that."

"It doesn't matter. What matters is you have the right to be happy, Pierre, and only you can make yourself that way. Don't rely on Gatian, or anyone else, to do it for you." Oliver twirled the flower between his fingers. "I was never going to be anything except a whore, but I made the best of the situation. I read all the books Gatian brought me, and he talked to me about his travels. You can change your place in the world. You can become a part of the world where I was hidden away."

Nodding, Pierre stood and wandered to where a small fountain spilled water into a basin. He dangled his fingers into the cool water. "Did you love him?"

The silence grew around them until Pierre thought Oliver might have disappeared. He glanced over his shoulder to where the man sat. Oliver was still there, still playing with the rose, and he had tears running down his cheeks.

"Yes, I did. He asked me to leave with him. To go and travel the world as his lover and companion, but I turned him down. I think he thought it was because I didn't love him or I liked my life as it was."

"It wasn't?"

Oliver shook his head. "No. I did care deeply for him. Was it love? I don't know. I was a whore. How would I know what love was? I didn't go with him because I didn't want him to be shunned by his peers because he took up with a whore. I cared too much to let him ruin his life like that."

Pierre looked back into the water and said, "Did he know that?"

"I tried telling him, but I'm not sure he believed me."

"Do you know what he did to revenge what happened to you?" Pierre kept playing in the water. "He cared so much about you, he had to seek justice for you, even if the man who killed you wasn't punished openly."

"I know. I saw what he did. I've been hanging around since I died. I wish I could have done something to help save him when he was killed." Oliver sighed. "I have to go. If you get the chance, will you tell him I did care for him? I wish I could have gone traveling with him, but I didn't want to destroy his life."

"If I see him again, I'll tell him."

Pierre turned to see Oliver set the rose down on the bench and slowly disappear. He wandered back over, picked up the flower and smelled it. As the scent filled his nose, the world around him went black.

* * * *

Pierre sat up with a gasp. His heart raced, and he couldn't seem to catch his breath. He looked around, searching the room for the sight of Oliver or something. Faint light came in through the curtains, alerting him to the rising sun.

"Wow," he whispered as he climbed out of bed and walked to the bathroom. He got a drink of water before wandering back. "It felt so real, even though I knew it was a dream. It had to be a dream. Oliver's dead."

As Pierre started to crawl under the covers, he spotted something on the pillow next to his. He picked up the rose with his trembling hand. Pierre stared at it, knowing it hadn't been there when he went to sleep. How had it gotten there? He very much doubted Johnson would have snuck in to leave it. The butler didn't seem to be the sneaking type.

Could Death have come in and left it? He shook his head. While Death did seem the type to leave romantic gestures like the rose, Pierre figured the Horseman would have simply joined him in bed if he'd gotten back already.

Lying down, Pierre held the rose in his fingers and thought about what Oliver had said. The ghost was right about Pierre having the chance to change his world. All Pierre needed to do was apologize to his parents and start working on making himself a better person. He could do it. All he had to do was think about what kind of man Death would want. Death wouldn't want an addict or a man who valued himself so cheaply that he allowed himself to be used for drugs or status.

Pierre dozed off for a little while, waking again when his alarm went off. After taking a shower and getting dressed, he carried his bag downstairs, taking the rose with him. Johnson stood at the bottom of the stairs.

"You can leave your bag here, sir. I'll make sure it gets in the car. I took the liberty of ensuring breakfast was ready for you. Master Almasia wouldn't be happy if I let you leave hungry."

"We both know he's not going to be happy you let me leave period, Johnson." Pierre clapped the man on the shoulder as he went by.

"It won't be the first time he's been angry with me," Johnson admitted, gesturing to a footman to serve Pierre his plate.

"I'm going to leave him a note on the desk in the study. Can you make sure he gets it?" Pierre took a sip of coffee.

"Certainly, sir. I must say we will miss you here. Master Almasia has been the happiest I've ever seen him while in your company." Johnson bowed slightly before leaving the room.

Smiling, Pierre settled in to eat the massive amount of food the cook had put on his plate. While his heart sang at Johnson's words about Death being happy with him, Pierre knew the truth. It didn't matter if Death loved him or not, they couldn't be together. Death was the Pale Rider, the last of the Horsemen, and the most important one. Pierre couldn't interfere with Death's job, no matter how much he might want to.

After finishing, he headed to the study where he found some paper and a pen waiting for him. He sat and composed his thoughts before starting to write. He ignored the tears, even when they splashed down and smeared the ink.

Pierre folded the paper, stuck it in an envelope, and wrote 'Death' on the front. He propped it up against the pencil holder for Johnson to find. Pierre went to the window, looking out over the gardens toward the fountain where he'd talked to Oliver in his dream.

Was there something magical about the house? Could it make dreams real, or had Oliver simply wanted to talk to him badly enough the ghost created the situation? Either way, Pierre was glad he'd had a chance to talk to Oliver, and actually see the man Death loved.

"Sir, your car is here," Johnson spoke from the doorway.

"Thank you, Johnson."

They strolled down the hall together, and Pierre shook Johnson's hand before leaving. As the chauffeur drove down the driveway one last time, Pierre turned to look back, committing the picture of the country home silhouetted against the blue sky to his memory. He inserted Death into the image, standing at the top of the front steps like he waited for Pierre to come home.

Pierre would use those images to help him when things got tough. He wasn't stupid enough to believe he could rejoin the real world without some struggles, but he was willing to do everything he had to do not to become the addict he was before.

"Bye, Death," Pierre whispered as the house vanished from view. "Maybe we'll meet again sometime, and I can tell you how much I care."

Facing forwards, Pierre took a deep breath and touched one velvety petal of the rose he carried.

Chapter Eleven

Whirling, Death opened his mouth to shout at Johnson, but closed it when he saw the expression on his long-time employee's face. Johnson hadn't been happy about letting Pierre go, but short of locking him up like a prisoner, there was nothing Johnson could have done.

Death sighed and scrubbed his hands through his hair. "I'm sorry, Johnson. I know you couldn't keep him locked up here. I'd just hoped he would've stuck around, so we could talk."

Johnson nodded. "Understandable, sir. He did leave you a note. I left it on your desk in your personal study."

"Thank you, Johnson. Could you have a tray delivered to my sitting room? I don't feel like eating in the dining room alone tonight."

"Certainly, sir."

Death removed his jacket and hung it up before wandering out onto the veranda. He leaned against the railing, staring out over the gardens. The roses were blooming, and he smiled at the riot of reds, yellows, whites and pinks. It had taken him years to get the gardens landscaped the way he wanted. The roses had been Oliver's favorite flowers, and Death had wanted to honor him in some way that would be around for as long as possible.

A soft knock brought him back into his room, and he called out for the footman to come in. The man set the tray down on Death's desk and bowed slightly before leaving. After changing into jeans and T-shirt, he wandered into his sitting room and took a seat behind his desk.

He spotted the note Johnson said Pierre had left for him. Death reached out to finger the edges of the envelope. Did he want to read it right now? Should he wait until after he ate? Snorting, he grabbed the note and stood. He didn't really need to eat, so he could ignore the food.

After moving to the couch, he sat in the corner and stared at the note. Why was he so reluctant to open it? It wasn't like he and Pierre had had an argument or something before Death had left. Johnson said Pierre wasn't angry when he'd left. He simply seemed determined to begin his life again.

A thought hit him, and he reached over to grab his laptop out of his case. He turned it on, leaning his head back while he waited for the screen to come up. Had Pierre stayed on the wagon and managed to keep sober? Was he surrounding himself with people who cared about him for who he was and not what he could get them?

He brought up his web browser and typed in Pierre's name. Images and articles began popping up. It had been three days since Death had last seen Pierre, and he worried the mortal had been sucked back into his old crowd.

Death read the articles, and a smile grew on his face. It seemed the prodigal son had returned home. The news reported Pierre coming home, spending his first night back with his family, and then the next day going to work with Jameson Robertson at Fortescue International Headquarters in London.

"Good for you, Pierre," Death murmured as he cleared his browser and shut down his laptop. He wasn't doing any more work for the night.

After returning the laptop to its case, Death picked up the envelope and opened it. He grinned at Pierre's handwriting, spidery and wild, not staying on the line. There were spots where the ink was smudged, and he studied those. Were those tearstains? Had Pierre been crying while he wrote the letter?

He took a deep breath and began to read. When he'd finished, he folded the paper back up and returned it to its envelope. Death set it down on the end table and pushed to his feet, wandering back into his bedroom. He pulled out a pair of tennis shoes and put them on.

The sun was setting as he made his way out into the gardens, slowly strolling down one path and another until he found himself at the small fountain and the bench beside a bed of blooming red roses. After sitting, Death plucked a rose from a bush and twirled it around in his fingers like he'd seen Oliver do a hundred times.

"You talked to him in a dream, huh?"

Death didn't care what his sitting out in the garden talking to himself might look like to the servants. He wanted answers and he hoped Oliver would be willing to give them to him. Yet for some reason, there didn't seem to be any presence in the area like there had been all the times before when Death had come to sit on the bench. He only just acknowledged its being there by its absence.

"Have you left me? Was talking to Pierre your last chance to make me admit you were around? Why didn't you talk to me before this?"

Nothing, and Death didn't understand why Oliver wasn't around anymore. It wasn't like Pierre knew Oliver or would've even been able to comprehend what Oliver had gone through in his young life.

"But they did have something in common."

Death managed not to jump when Lam's voice drifted in from behind him. He twisted on the bench to meet the angel's gaze.

"What might that have been?"

"They both loved you." Lam joined him without waiting for permission.

"Both of them left me. If Oliver had loved me, he would have run off with me. I didn't care what society thought of us. We could have traveled around the world, and no one would have known any different about our relationship." Death tossed the flower at Lam. "Pierre should have waited for me to come back. I would have told him how I felt about him, but he left to return to his own world."

After sniffing it, Lam sneezed and set the rose to the side. "You're a bastard, Death. You know that, right? You've always been an arrogant asshole."

Death shot Lam a surprised glance. "Such language from one of God's creatures. You've been hanging out with someone in particular too much."

"Shut up." Lam punched him on the arm. "Listen to yourself. Oliver left you because he was killed, jackass. It wasn't like he wanted to get strangled to death by some bastard. Pierre went home, so he could grow up and take his place at the head of the family empire. That's damn selfish of him, isn't it?"

Death leaned forward, resting his elbows on his thighs while letting his hands dangle between his knees. "I know I'm a bastard. I've been told that many times by hundreds of people. Nothing you say is news to me. I let Oliver down, Lam. I wasn't there like I should have been when he died."

"True, he might not have died that night if you were there, but you couldn't be with him every minute of every day, Death. You have no idea why he was killed, and it might have been something that would have happened eventually anyway. He was a whore, Death, and their life expectancies were never very long to begin with during those times."

Death hated the fact Lam was right. He'd always known somewhere deep in his brain, Oliver's death wasn't his fault. He might have postponed it, but at some point and some time, it would have happened. One thing being the Pale Rider taught him was that no one escaped Death. No mortal got to choose his time of death or how he died. Well, unless he committed suicide, but for the most part, the endings of their lives were pre-destined.

"Why did Pierre leave then?"

Lam shrugged. "What did his letter say?"

Death glared at the angel. "How did you know he wrote me a letter?"

"I started in your sitting room and spotted the note on the table. When I didn't find you there, I came out here." Lam nudged Death with his shoulder. "I don't rummage around your personal belongings."

"I know." Death rubbed his chin. "I'm just upset because while I loved Oliver, I never really had him in my life. Not like Pierre was for those weeks. Oliver was probably right to say no when I asked him to run away with me. We probably would never have survived it."

Lam stayed silent, and Death kept talking.

"Pierre didn't want to be a kept man. He wanted to start living and earning the money he spent. He knew if he stayed with me he wouldn't have to want for anything, but anything he got he wouldn't have worked for. He wanted to try and see what a normal life would be like."

"So it wasn't like he decided he didn't want anything more to do with you and just left. He had to go back to his life and make sure he could survive without the drugs and the groupies." Lam smiled. "I saw the news reports. Sounds like he isn't doing too badly."

"It's only been a few days, but I do think he's smart enough to handle the work. Oh, he'll make mistakes, yet I'm pretty sure he won't turn to drugs to fix the problems anymore."

Lam turned slightly, and Death looked him in the eye.

"Do you love him, Death?"

Taking a deep breath, Death thought about everything he'd done with Pierre. Not just the sex, which had been some of the best he'd ever had, but all the times in between when all they'd done was sit and talk. He'd learned Pierre had an intelligent mind when it wasn't dulled by the heroin. Did he love Pierre?

The knowledge he could never see Pierre again tore through his chest, and he gasped, pressing his hand to his heart. His answer was obvious in the pain.

"Yes, I do love him. It wasn't something I planned, Lam, and I know the rules. I can't have anything to do with him because he's mortal." Death snarled and jumped to his feet. "Why the hell did you let me take Pierre that night? What were you thinking?"

Lam laughed. "I was thinking he might be the one person who could save you from yourself, Death. You were so determined to feel guilty for something you couldn't prevent, and so determined not to feel any regret for killing the man who raped your sister."

"I don't regret St. Lucian's death. He raped Emilia, and from what I found out about him, he would have done it again to another innocent woman. I stopped a serial rapist, even though I didn't know what that was back then." Death wouldn't feel guilt for St. Lucian's death.

"True. So I guess I can't yell at you for that one. Have you accepted the truth about Oliver's death? You couldn't have stopped it or done anything to keep it from happening."

Death nodded. "By letting go of my guilt, I let go of him. Is that why I can't hear him anymore?"

The angel shrugged. "Maybe. I don't know anything about that, but I do know this. You're finally free, Gatian Almasia. Live out your mortal life and try to find love along the way."

Death's mouth dropped open as Lam disappeared. He went to the fountain and stared at his reflection in the water. His hair was no longer pale ash gray. It was the black he remembered from when he was mortal. There were a few strands of silver streaking it, but a man of his age would normally have those. His eyes were dark blue, so dark that they looked black, yet he could see the pupils and irises.

"What is the meaning of this, Lam?" he shouted into the sky.

"It means you are free, Gatian. You are mortal like your former fellow Horsemen. If you love Pierre, go and find him. Tell him how much you do care for him, and live your lives together. Being able to spend every minute with the one you love is truly a gift from God."

Lam's voice played on the wind, holding happiness and sorrow intermingled. Death wanted to shout in triumph, but he bit his lip. While Lam might not be around, it still didn't seem right to celebrate his being able to find Pierre and confess his love when Lam couldn't have anything to do with the being he loved.

"Thank you," he whispered.

A gentle breeze ruffled his hair before Gatian turned and headed back to the house. He'd get some sleep tonight, than set about re-entering the world. After that, he'd go in search of Pierre and see if the mortal would still be interested in dating Gatian Almasia, the man formerly known as Death.

* * * *

Pierre looked over the crowd of well-dressed people and smiled. He sipped his whiskey as he mingled, never staying too long with any group. He'd been in meetings all day for Fortescue International, and hadn't had time to do any research on the charity the party was for. It was one of many his corporation supported, but Pierre had found over the months of slowly learning the business, he hated not being prepared.

"Did you hear who might be coming tonight?"

He smiled as his mother rested her hand in the crook of his elbow. "No, Mother. I wasn't privy to the guest list. What marvelous patron might be gracing us with his or her presence?"

"Stop teasing." She smacked him on the chest. "Jameson told me he's never accepted an invitation before."

Pierre glanced over to where his stepfather stood, schmoozing another group of possible donors. Jameson met his eyes and nodded before looking back at the lady next to him.

When Pierre had arrived back home four months ago, he hadn't been sure what his reception would be like. His mother had cried and yelled at him the whole time she'd hugged the stuffing out of him. Jameson had cried as well but he hadn't shouted. He'd met Pierre's gaze and must have seen something in Pierre's eyes that had told him Pierre was different.

He'd explained to Jameson how sorry he was at how he'd acted since Jameson had married Pierre's mom. He'd explained what he wanted to achieve with the business, and Jameson had welcomed him with open arms. In the months since then, Pierre had gotten a crash course in running an international business. He was still learning, but Jameson told him he had the ability to be a top-notch CEO.

"Are you listening to me, Pierre?"

"Yes, Mom. Who has you all in a twitter?" He silently laughed because he'd never seen his mother act so star-struck about anyone, not even the Queen of England.

"Gatian Almasia." If his mother were less dignified, she would've been clapping her hands together like a little child on Christmas Day.

He stumbled to a halt, almost spilling his drink all over the latest celebutante. He didn't know who she was or what she was famous for. After setting his drink down on one of the nearby tables, he grabbed his mom's arms and shook her slightly.

"Did you say Gatian Almasia RSVP'd for this event?"

"Yes." His mother studied him. "I didn't realize you knew him. He's never been seen at parties or even out in public for years. How did you meet him?"

"I didn't meet him. I've just heard so much about him. It would great to meet the man who has managed to run a billion dollar business while being a recluse."

Pierre didn't know how Death would want to play it, if they did meet.

A low murmur moved through the crowd, and people fell silent as a tall, dark-haired man stepped into the room. Pierre's mouth went dry, and he thought his heart was going to burst from his chest.

After accepting the fact he would never be able to see Death again, he couldn't believe the man strolled through the gaping crowd straight toward him and his mother. She squeezed his arm so tightly he thought all the circulation had been cut off, though he totally understood her excitement. Christ, he wanted to throw himself into Death's arms and say aloud everything he'd written in the note.

"Mrs. Robertson, it's a pleasure to finally meet you. I have heard wonderful things about you."

Death took Pierre's mother's hand in his and brushed her knuckles with his lips. She giggled and blushed like a giddy schoolgirl. Pierre couldn't help but smile at her joy. Jameson joined them as others gathered around.

"Mr. Almasia, it's a true honor to have you join us tonight. We know you don't attend many events." Jameson held out his hand, and Death shook it.

"I couldn't pass up the opportunity. I've also heard the Fortescue Charitable Foundation puts on quite a party."

Death turned his gaze on Pierre, and Pierre gasped. Where Death's eyes had been pure black the last time Pierre had seen him, now they were dark blue with noticeable pupils. The man's hair wasn't the pale gray Pierre remembered either, but black streaked with silver.

"Mr. Fortescue, it's marvelous to finally meet you as well. I was quite intrigued when I was told you were stepping into your grandfather's footsteps. You'll have big shoes to fill."

Pierre licked his lips, and the way Death's eyes flared with heat at the gesture caused Pierre's cock to harden. God, he couldn't get an erection in the middle of the charity event, especially not with his mother right next to him.

"Good evening, Mr. Almasia. I have to say I'm surprised to see you here. I didn't think you went out much."

Their hands touched, and it felt like electricity raced from their palms to Pierre's groin. He really wanted to throw himself into Death's arms and beg Death to fuck him. Not the most proper thing he could do.

"I didn't, but a change in my circumstances has allowed me to move more freely in society from now on." Death looked over at Pierre's mother and stepfather. "May I borrow Pierre for a few minutes? I have a business proposition I'd like to discuss with him."

Jameson's eyes lit up at the possibility of Fortescue International doing business with Almasia Corporation. "Of course. In fact, if you would like more privacy, you're welcome to use one of our board rooms."

"Or maybe we could just retire to Pierre's office," Death suggested, glancing at Pierre.

Pierre cleared his throat. "Certainly. If you'll follow me, sir."

"Please, call me Gatian."

Pierre led the way through the crowd, very conscious of Death's hand resting at the small of his back. Silence settled around them as they headed down the hallway toward Pierre's office.

"Pierre, wait a moment."

He stiffened at the sound of Lars' voice. If he'd known Lars had been invited, he would have had his invitation revoked, but he hadn't had a chance to look at the guest list. Pierre would have ignored Lars, but Death stopped and turned.

"What do you want, Lars?" Pierre stared daggers at his former lover.

"I hoped I could get a chance to talk to Mr. Almasia. I gave one of his associates some information a few months ago on a good business deal. I wanted to know how well it went, and if maybe my finder's fee got lost in the mail."

Lars' smile didn't strike Pierre as charming anymore. It seemed oily and creepy, like Lars was trying too hard to come across as friendly and nice. Pierre studied his former lover and realized the alcohol and drugs must have clouded his judgment. Now that Pierre was sober and clean, there was no way he'd come with ten feet of Lars, and he definitely he wouldn't sleep with the man.

"God, I'm a complete idiot," Pierre muttered.

Death snorted but kept his gaze on Lars. Pierre watched while Lars seemed to shrink into himself under Death's cold stare. The uncomfortable silence grew until it was thick enough Pierre could have cut it with a knife.

"Mr. Holden, because this is a charity event, I'm willing to put my animosity toward you aside at the moment. You won't be receiving any finder's fee, and tomorrow, expect to be served with a subpoena. You're being charged with insider trading, and my colleague is the one to testify against you." Death took a step toward Lars, leaning in close to his ear. "And you tossed away something very precious, which I will appreciate much more than you ever did."

Lars' gaze darted to Pierre, and the dawning expression of shock and disgust told Pierre Lars had figured out the relationship between Gatian and him. "Were you letting him fuck you as well, Pierre? How much did he pay you for your ass?"

The venom in Lars' voice surprised Pierre, causing him to take a step back. Death slid over, blocking Lars' view of Pierre, but Pierre wasn't going to let Death fight his battles for him. No more running away from his problems.

Pierre touched Death on the shoulder, and when Death glanced at him, he smiled to let him know he was okay. Death inclined his head while stepping aside.

"I wasn't fucking him while we were together, Lars. Of course, you have no room to talk since you went and got married to a girl on the same weekend you were supposed to be meeting me in Paris. I'm not the one who gave a young kid his first shot of heroin, and his first drink when he was eighteen."

Death growled and grabbed Lars. "You were the one who got Pierre hooked on heroin? Why?"

Lars stuttered, his feet barely touching the ground as Death shook him.

"I know why. He did it to get me hooked, and so I'd do anything to get more, including let him fuck me. Lars Holden doesn't have any money of his own, and the best way to keep the life he's accustomed to living is by having someone addicted to something he can provide."

Death tossed Lars away from him like he was trash. "How much is your wife worth? What did you get her addicted to?"

Pierre wrinkled his nose as he thought back to the photographs he'd seen of the wedding. "Your wife is Janice Klauson, the only daughter of Heinrich Klauson, one of Germany's richest manufacturers. I do believe she is addicted to crystal meth and coke. Guess you made sure she re-did her will to name you beneficiary of her money."

"I love you, Pierre. I made a mistake, but I want you back. You're the only one I love." Lars tried to get closer to Pierre.

Pierre stepped toward Death, and Death encircled Pierre's waist to pull him closer. Pierre shook his head.

"Ah, Lars. Is Janice going to divorce you or did her daddy get wind of what you did, and took control of her money? Either way, you're screwed, because you also like to gamble, and I'm betting you owe some dangerous men a lot of money." Pierre glanced at Death and chuckled. "Maybe you should invite Lars to play poker with you, Gatian. He's not a good card player, or dice thrower, plus he can't pick a winner at the race track if his life depended on it."

"I don't gamble," Death said. He let go of Pierre and walked closer to Lars. "I will tell you this, Holden. Stay far away from Pierre as you possibly can. If I see you sniffing around him, I'll take you out, and I don't mean killing you. I'll make you wish you were dead."

Lars' eyes grew wide at the coldness in Death's voice, and like Lars, Pierre could hear the truth in the words. Considering what Pierre knew Death had done to the man who'd killed Oliver, Pierre didn't doubt Death would do what he'd said.

"Get out of here and don't come back."

After whirling around, Lars practically ran from them like his ass was on fire. Pierre looked up at Death and laughed.

"Wow. You're good with the scary eyes."

Death shrugged. "It helps that I meant every word I said to him. I'll ruin his life if he comes near you again."

Pierre shivered, and his heart soared a little. He'd never had anyone seem so determined to protect him. After taking Death's hand, he led the man to his office. The door had barely shut and Pierre found himself pinned to it with Death kissing him.

There wasn't any talking to be done at the moment. All either one of them wanted was to be as close to each other as possible. Their clothes fell in piles on the floor at their feet. Maybe Pierre should have been more concerned for the expensive suit his mother had picked out for him. All he could think about was getting Death inside him as quickly as possible.

He started to drop to his knees, but Death caught him and their eyes met.

"No. If you put your mouth on me, I'll come, and I don't want to do that until my cock is in your ass."

"So romantic," Pierre teased.

Death rolled his eyes. "I love you, Pierre, and I want you. Can we talk about the rest of it afterwards?"

Death loved him? Stunned, Pierre could only nod. He stumbled slightly as Death dragged him over to the leather couch against one of the office walls.

"Do you have anything in here we can use for lube?"

"You mean you didn't come prepared?" Pierre removed his hand from Death's tight grip and wandered over to his desk. "I have some hand lotion. It's not quite as good as lube, but it'll work in a pinch."

Death caught the bottle when Pierre tossed it to him. "Good. I didn't fancy having to run out to the nearest store to get some."

Pierre knelt on the couch, tilting his ass out to entice Death closer. Death stroked his hand down Pierre's spine, teasing the soft skin at the small of his back for a second before continuing to rub his finger over Pierre's opening. Pierre sighed in happiness at having Death with him again.

"You've done well for yourself," Death complimented him.

Resting his head on the back of the couch, Pierre moaned softly when Death eased the tip of one finger inside. He couldn't respond to Death's observation, his mind and body being overcome by sensation and need. Pushing back, he took more of Death inside, almost begging for the man to fuck him. He knew it wouldn't happen until Death was sure Pierre was stretched enough.

Death leaned over and kissed Pierre's back. "I've missed you."

Pierre whimpered and got lost in both the touch of Death's lips and fingers. Death kissed along the line of Pierre's back while fingering him open. One. Two. Pierre lost track of how many fingers were stretching him. Suddenly, they were gone, and so was Death's warmth along his back.

"Wait. Please, Death, fuck me. I need you."

"I know, honey. Come here." Death supported him while he turned, lying back on the couch and facing Death. "I want to see your face when I make love to you this time."

"Okay." Pierre blinked as he watched Death settled between his legs, as naked as the day he was born. "I've missed you so much."

"We don't have to be alone anymore, Pierre. I promise."

Death positioned the head of his cock at Pierre's opening. Their eyes met and locked when Death sank into Pierre. There was a little bit of a burn at the beginning, but Pierre relaxed and breathed through the pressure. Finally, Death was buried all the way in, and they both froze for a moment.

"Welcome home," Pierre whispered to Death.

Tears welled in Death's eyes before he blinked and started moving. After reaching up, Pierre gripped Death's shoulders, riding each thrust with every atom of his body. He wanted to bring so much pleasure to Death, so that the Horseman didn't regret coming to find him.

Their lovemaking became a dance of give and take, moving together in perfect harmony. The pleasure and need grew, swirling between them and binding them closer together with each stroke in and slow slide out. Pierre cried out every time Death nailed his gland, and his blood pounded in his ears as desire shot through him, pooling in his balls.

"Death, I'm going to come soon," he warned.

"My name is Gatian. I want to hear you say it as you come," Death ordered him while he sped up, driving Pierre closer and closer to the summit of his climax.

"Gatian," Pierre cried out, his cum splashing from his cock, coating his stomach, and some even hitting his chest.

Death grunted and slammed in, freezing when he flooded Pierre's ass with his seed. They stayed in their spots, trembling and panting until neither was in danger of passing out. Death dropped his head forward, resting it on Pierre's forehead. Their breaths mingled together, and Pierre swore their hearts began to beat at the same pace.

"We should probably clean up. I'm not entirely sure I locked the door," he suggested once he figured he could get his muscles to respond to orders.

"Okay."

They groaned when Death slid from him. He accepted Death's hand and let him pull him off the couch. He led the way into his private bathroom where they cleaned up before heading back out to dress.

When they were properly attired again, they sat on the couch, and Pierre took a deep breath.

"What are you doing here? I thought we weren't going to be able to see each other anymore since you're a Horseman and all that."

Death took his hand and waited until he looked at him. "Do you love me, Pierre?"

Pierre licked his lips and nodded. "Yes. I do, but I couldn't stay there with you. I don't want to be a kept man. I think I'd probably end being addicted again because I couldn't handle the boredom."

"I know that. I understand why you left, though I'll admit I wasn't happy at first. It felt like neither you nor Oliver wanted to be with me." Grinning, Death shook his head. "I do believe my pride was injured."

"Oliver didn't go with you when you asked because he cared so much about you. He didn't want you to be shunned by society for taking up with a whore. It wasn't because he didn't love you or anything like that." Pierre had to tell Death what Oliver had told him in his dream. He wanted to make sure he delivered the message first.

"I think I always knew that, but still my pride was hurt. It was easier to believe Oliver didn't love me, than to accept the responsibility of how much I meant to him." Death shook his head again. "Anyway, because I've finally come to terms with my own guilt over Oliver's death, I've been freed from being a Horseman."

"Really?" Pierre couldn't help the excitement welling up inside him.

Death smiled and brought Pierre's hand up to his lips, brushing a kiss over his knuckles. "Yes. I'm as mortal as you are now. I came here tonight to find out if you'd be interested in going out on a date with me."

"A date?" Pierre thought about what they'd just done. "Aren't we past the dating stage by now?"

"No. We became lovers when I was a Horseman. Now we're going to get to know each other since I'm mortal. There's nothing to keep us apart anymore, Pierre. I love you and want to spend the rest of my mortal life with you."

Pierre studied Death's beautiful dark blue eyes and smiled. "All right. We'll start over then."

"Perfect."

Death stood and bowed slightly. "I'd like to introduce myself. My name is Gatian Almasia, and I'm looking forward to getting to know you, Mr. Pierre Fortescue."

Epilogue

Lam stood in the wasteland, waiting for the newest Horseman to arrive. He didn't pace or fidget since angels didn't do those things. No, he simply crouched, staring out over the black expanse, and wondered how Gatian and Pierre were doing.

He admitted to himself that there had been a few occasions when he'd thought Gatian would never find someone to love. If ever there was a man caught up in the past, it was Gatian, and it had been difficult to find the right mortal for him. Yet the moment Lam had seen Pierre, the angel had known he was perfect for Gatian.

"Turns out you were right."

He straightened and whirled, glaring at Day who stood behind him.

"You aren't supposed to be here," he reminded his lover.

Day shrugged. "I'm not supposed to do a lot of things I do. So far no one's come to stop me."

"One day they will."

And the thought of that day terrified Lam, because there wouldn't be anything he could do to stop them when they chose to end Day's life.

Day stepped closer to him and cradled Lam's face in his hands. "Don't worry about me, love. If or when it happens, I'll deal with it like I always do."

A crack of lightning lit the sky, and Lam winced. Day looked over Lam's shoulder and grimaced.

"It's time for you to get back to work, love. Go help the poor confused bastard. Don't you ever get tired of helping them out? Of dealing with their anger and their questions?"

"It's my job, Day. I don't have a choice, and I'm one of the more patient angels. At least I'll take the time to answer them."

Day snorted. "Most of your fellow angels have a high opinion of themselves. How are Gatian and Pierre doing?"

Lam leaned forwards, placing a quick kiss on Day's lips. "Gatian and Pierre are in love and happy together. I can't help being happy for them."

Day grimaced, and there was a hint of sadness in Lam's lover's eyes, but he gave Lam a little hug before pushing him away. "Go do your job, Lam."

As Lam walked away, Day's voice drifted to him on a strange little breeze.

"Someday we'll be happy and together without anyone judging us."

* * * *

Four years later

Gatian narrowed his eyes while tugging on the sleeves of his dress shirt. "I can't believe I let you talk me into inviting them for the wedding."

His soon-to-be husband peered around the bathroom doorframe to grin at him. "Come on. You and I both know that there's no way you would've agreed unless you wanted to see them. I just gave you a little push to send those invites out."

Grunting, he pulled on his vest then buttoned it. He didn't answer Pierre, mostly because the man was right. As much as Gatian wanted to pretend he wasn't curious about the others, he couldn't hide it from Pierre, who knew him too well.

"I didn't think they'd accept. None of them knew my mortal name. Do you think they've figured out I'm human again?"

"They're curious, just like you are. They agreed to come because they want to find out if you're mortal or if you're throwing caution to the wind and not worrying about the consequences." Pierre reached out to straighten Gatian's tie and smiled. "You might be surprised. You all could become friends out of this."

He let Pierre tweak his clothes, not really interested in how he looked at the moment. His mind kept chasing back to the fact that in a matter of minutes, the other three former Horsemen would be in his apartment and he'd have to interact with them on equal footing. That had never happened before.

Pierre gave him a quick peck on the cheek. "Quit worrying. I know you've only dealt with them when you were the *de facto* leader, but you don't have to do that anymore. Being on equal footing might help."

"I don't need friends. I have you." He encircled Pierre's waist then tugged him close before kissing him hard.

He smiled when Pierre opened to him and allowed him to sweep his tongue into his mouth, teasing and stroking. Their breathy pants mingled as the lust fired between them. Gatian slid his hands down Pierre's back to grab his ass.

"Oh," Pierre gasped, letting his head drop back so Gatian could nibble along his throat. "We don't have time for this. Our guests will be arriving any minute now."

"I don't care," he muttered, far more interested in getting Pierre naked and in bed.

Pierre wiggled and pushed hard enough that Gatian had to let him go. "You can fuck me later. I want to meet Aldo again and find out what the others are like. As much as I love the fact you're that into me and I'm your whole world, you do need other friends. Broaden your horizons a little."

Gatian stared at Pierre. "Broaden my horizons? I've been on this earth for several centuries. I think my horizons are as broad as they're going to get."

"Oh...honey, you have no idea about all the things you still have to learn." Pierre winked before dashing out of the room.

"You're a brat," Gatian yelled as he followed Pierre out to the living room. He skidded to a halt when he saw the other people standing there.

Pierre flashed him a quick smile before approaching Aldo. "I do remember you, Doctor. Thank you so much for coming."

Aldo shook Pierre's hand then introduced Bart. "This is my husband, Bart. I appreciate the invitation, though I will admit I was surprised to get one."

"Well, I wanted Gatian to have some friends at the ceremony. My family and friends will be there, but he doesn't have any. I think you're more family than friends to him, since you have all known each other for so long." Pierre faced the other men. "And you are?"

"I'm Baqir and this is my husband, Russ. I was formerly the Red Horseman, War." Baqir shook Pierre's hand then motioned to Russ. "You are Pierre Fortsecue, right?"

Pierre nodded. "Yes, I am."

Gatian couldn't turn around and leave, not when they'd all seen him. He took a deep breath before joining Pierre. "Baqir, it's good to see you again. Being mortal agrees with you."

Baqir eyed him, but only nodded. "I'm enjoying my life."

"Good." He saw Kibwe studying him. "Kibwe, you look good as well. Still living in the jungle?"

Kibwe sniffed. "Where else would we live? Neither Ekundayo nor I are meant to live in the city."

Ekundayo nudged Kibwe then greeted Gatian. "Ignore him, Mr. Almasia. Congratulations on your engagement."

"Please, call me Gatian, and he's Pierre. You're all the closest thing I have to family, so there's no point in standing on ceremony. Also, thank you. I truly am glad you came."

Pierre's approval rolled over him, and Gatian couldn't help the smile crossing his face. It was kind of pathetic in a way. He used to be the most feared of the Horsemen, and now his own happiness depended on the man he loved. If Pierre wasn't happy, Gatian would do everything in his power to bring joy back to him.

Kibwe didn't look convinced, but Gatian went to meet the other men. He shook their hands then offered them drinks. Pierre strolled among the couples, chatting with them while Gatian worked on the refreshments.

Baqir joined him at the bar. "You look good, Gatian. Are you mortal again?"

"Yes." He handed Baqir his glass of whiskey. "I'm glad about that, though I'd already decided not to give Pierre up, even if I didn't turn back."

"Now you know how each of us felt when we met the men we loved," Baqir pointed out.

He sighed. "I do, but at the time, I didn't believe love was possible for us. Yet each time one of you found the perfect guy for you, it gave me a little more hope."

"And now you're getting married," Aldo spoke as he took his drink from the tray.

"Never thought that would happen," Gatian muttered and Aldo snorted.

"If you'd stayed alive the first time, it wouldn't have. The world is more enlightened now," Aldo said.

Kibwe wandered over to where they stood. The former Horsemen watched as their husbands and Gatian's fiancé got to know each other. Gatian looked at each man then smiled. Pierre was right. He'd been through centuries' worth of strife and danger with these men. They were the closest things he had to family. Maybe he should make a bigger effort to get to know them.

"I really do want to thank you for coming," he announced. "I'd like to make a toast."

Everyone faced him, and Gatian lifted his glass.

"To family created over time instead of through blood." Then he met Pierre's shining gaze. "To believing love can change a person's destiny."

About the Author

There is beauty in every kind of love, so why not live a life without boundaries? Experiencing everything the world offers fascinates T.A. and writing about the things that make each of us unique is how she shares those insights. When not writing, T.A.'s watching movies, reading and living life to the fullest.

T.A. Chase loves to hear from readers. You can find her contact information, website and author biography at http://www.pride-publishing.com.